Nicole Lobry de Bruyn is 36 years old and has been writing fiction for ten years. This is her first novel. She studied creative writing at Murdoch University under Marion Campbell. She is also a qualified veterinarian. Nicole lives in Fremantle, Western Australia, with her partner Graham Miller and their Burmese cat and French Bulldog.

Undertow

Nicole Lobry de Bruyn

ALLEN & UNWIN

First published in 2001

Allen & Unwin
83 Alexander Street
Crows Nest NSW 2065
Australia
Phone: (61 2) 8425 0100
Fax: (61 2) 9906 2218
Email: frontdesk@allen-unwin.com.au
Web: http://www.allenandunwin.com

National Library of Australia
Cataloguing-in-Publication entry:

Lobry de Bruyn, Nicole, 1964– .
    Undertow.

    ISBN 1 86508 476 X.

    I. Title

A823.4

Set in 11 pt Garamond by Chapter 8 Pty Ltd
Printed by Australian Print Group, Maryborough, Victoria

10 9 8 7 6 5 4 3 2 1

To my family
Alex, June and Lisa

'It is longing that moves the sea.'
— Anne Michaels, *Fugitive Pieces*

Sometimes I imagine I am a dog paddling in the water. I stick my chin over the surface so it laps my neck. I pull my arms down through the clear aqua liquid as if they are the dog's front legs. I clench my fists so they resemble the inefficient paws. I feel the weight of my body barely afloat. I imagine the sea-sodden fur, heavy like wet wool. I let the water come over my mouth and nose, level with my eyes. I see ocean, blurry blues. Horizon and sea merge. I let myself sink without a struggle, but the air in my lungs keeps me near the surface. I try breathing out till all the air is gone; till all the alveoli have closed up. I picture them like bubble-wrap being trod on. Pop pop. When I can't stand it any more I surface and take a long breath.

In 1978 I am fourteen. It is a hideous age. I'm neither a child nor an adult, neither a woman nor a girl. Small red pimples dot my face and my father thinks I'm too young to shave my legs. Some girls my age have had sex while others are still obsessed with horses. I don't belong to either group. Boys and sex form a spiralling conversation between me and my friends, but I only take part to be polite. I haven't considered myself in the act. It is something I imagine happening to someone who doesn't look like me. She has a woman's hips and doesn't bite her nails; her hair isn't parted down the middle and held off her face by steel-grey bobby pins. I believe I'm grown-up thinking this way. I tell the others it is something to do when you are in love and not before. It's about spending a lifetime together; about you going blind and him going deaf; you being his ears and him your eyes. These are the ideas we circle through at lunch times while we sit on the smooth quadrangle lawn, my friends suntanning their calves with their shoes and socks off. I sit with my legs crossed under the tent of my skirt.

The players in the story are my mum Billie, my dad Ted, my sister Alison, my mother's twin Aunt Bette (who looks nothing like her), and their mother Nanna Pearl. There are others but they don't seem to matter. No one impacts on me like my family. They are the ones that etch themselves deeply. Everyone else shimmies over the surface. Then there's Mrs Teasdale, but I'll get to her later.

My name is Catrina but I call myself Cat when my parents aren't around. Dad would throw a fit if he heard me introduce myself this way. He has a thing about nicknames and thinks people should be called by what's on their birth certificate. Alison is therefore Alison and never Ally or Al. I am always Catrina and sometimes, when he's in that kind of mood, it becomes *Catrina, my little ballerina* — making obvious my thick straight legs and big feet. Of course, my parents don't call each other by their names and this is something I've brought up in defence of my nickname. They are Darl and Darl. They say that when I'm married I can call myself what I like, but while I live under their roof I will live by their rules. It's like marriage will signify the start of everything, and life before pairing is simply rehearsal.

I say, *What kind of name is Catrina?* It sounds like I should be permanently in a frilly frock, with black patent leather shoes and socks with lace edging. *Oh yes, that's the kind of little girl we wanted,* they say, *and instead we have one that wants to be called Cat, like some stray tabby that lives off garbage.* It's a lighthearted conversation but still I'm left feeling misunderstood. I tell them it's okay for them, since their names aren't daggy. *Anyway, what kind of name is Billie for a girl?* I ask Mum. She says *her* mother was ahead of her time.

There's a dog too. He's a yellow Labrador in love with water. He's important because without him maybe none of it will turn out the way it does. If one thing is the cause, you could say it is Ben. If you want to look for a turning point, a fulcrum to the story, then think of the moment Ben lurches himself into the waves. I think he knows more than he can express. He is the type of animal that people say has

3

been here before, even if they don't believe in reincarnation. When I'm sad he puts his chin on my lap for me to stroke his head, as if he knows it is soothing to do so. Perhaps he knows what he's doing when he swims out towards the horizon and just keeps going.

I remember a time when I have no concept of place other than home. Maybe I'm four or five. I think the entire world is exactly like my world. I am a fixture of my time and place, so inextricably linked that to me summer is five months of long dry heat, trees are eucalypts with sad skinny leaves, the sky is a distant dome of blue, everybody can swim and back yards have chooks in one corner and an old outside dunny with a pull chain and a wooden door that bangs in the wind.

But at fourteen I start to pick up on the parochial nature of the small city of Perth. I can feel Perth clinging to the edge of a very large landmass and have heard it described as the most isolated city in the world. I feel Perth's remoteness as if it's my own; as if I'm precariously related to my life. Sometimes I feel perched outside myself, gripping and clawing to a crumbling surface. Things that I rely on no longer seem reliable. I start to wonder and dream about foreign places and speaking a different language. Sometimes I watch my parents talking to me and see their lips move but don't understand a thing. I twist the sounds inside my head so the words mutate and my parents become foreigners. My make-believe self that lives in Europe is the same unrecognisable woman that I see having sex. I, the fourteen-year-old Cat, stay in the concrete world of suburban Perth, riding my pushbike around the dull hot streets, having a Choc Wedge after the beach on Sundays and catching a noisy green bus to school along the highway. Growing inside me is a sense of the suburban nature of my life.

So far I've grown up with the stability of one mother, one father, one sister and one dog, living in the one ordinary house on a quarter-acre block in a suburb not far from the city. We have a large eucalypt in the back yard that is a source of chores for Alison and me; forever raking leaves and bark from the lawn, or being sent onto the roof to clean out gutters, our father steadying the ladder from below while my mother, with her hand over her eyes, says she can't bear to watch.

At thirty-five I can feel the difference between the suburb I live in and the one where I grew up. They are thirty minutes one another, yet I feel different here to the way I feel from there. When I drive up the highway to visit Billie, it's like going back in time. The trees are older, taller, greener, with more abundant leaves. The magpies and kookaburras are consistently full of voice. Trees are big enough to be called widow-makers and require lopping by specialist tree surgeons with chainsaws. You are guaranteed the sound of lawn-mowing on weekends and people still have old rose bushes in preference to over-flowering icebergs. There's a carpet of jacaranda flowers across the footpath. You can't smell the ocean or the sheep ships from her back door, or hear the sound of the train when the air's thin before the rain.

It's as if the place I grew up in seeped inside me and became part of my fibre, so that when I return there it vibrates. It recognises the smells and the sounds that embedded themselves in my childhood.

Mum says we are lucky that she and Dad are stable, as if the main ingredient to successful parenting is staying in one place. For her, moving around from town to town and from school to school meant having no friends, and if you didn't have friends you had no social life, and no social life meant no parties, and no parties meant no boys, and no boys meant no boyfriend, and no boyfriend meant no marriage, and no marriage meant no babies. She uses Aunt Bette as an example of how badly life can turn out for someone. *Imagine No Husband*, she says, as if Aunt Bette has a terminal illness.

For Billie, having children is her most important achievement. She gives long monologues on how she almost never met Dad and therefore never married, and how she thought she would end up being the oldest unmarried hairdresser in the world. Again she uses Aunt Bette as an example — *Poor Bette, still working when she's nearly fifty and still at home with Mum.* Alison says the fact that Aunt Bette is a career woman and relishes her job is lost on Billie.

When we are small Aunt Bette smells of chalk dust and the tips of her fingers have a faint pastel tint to them from working on the blackboard in her classroom. Her cardigans are sprinkled with the fine coloured powder that puffs out of the duster as she bangs it on the wooden verandah post at the end of the school day. She's my grade one teacher, like she was Alison's a couple of years before, and I feel special because the teacher is my aunt. But she never treats me differently from the rest of the class, and sometimes she even forgets my name. I wonder if she does this on purpose.

She gets to school early to draw a picture for our class on the board. Then she asks us to write about it. We have only just learnt the alphabet. To write a sentence takes half the day. She draws in great detail — seahorses and toadstools, mermaids and milking cows — but it never seems to bother her to erase her art at the end of the day. Her right forearm is thick from gripping the duster and rubbing till the board is black and shining. Sometimes the drawings are so beautiful I want to be able to keep them. I hold a piece of paper against them. I lean my body into them, my fingers pushing hard against the paper, my palm flat against the blackboard. When I peel the paper away, there is only a smear of chalk dust. The picture has gone.

Aunt Bette says the introduction of whiteboards ruined teaching, and for as long as she can she continues with her coloured chalk and wooden handled duster.

Aunt Bette's pupils love her. She's like the mother that some children don't have. A woman with a pillowy bosom from which emerges a hanky to blow a kid's nose. She shows children how to hold their pencil, in whatever hand they choose. She never smacks a child, even when it's the norm to use a ruler or throw a duster at a quivering-lipped six-year-old. We overhear Aunt Bette tell Mum that Mr Fitzharding, the grade five teacher, should be sacked for what he did to that child, and afterwards are forever fearful of him, even though we don't know what it was he did. Billie says she always thought Mr Fitzharding a handsome man, and adds that she's surprised he never married. *Surely he must be thirty-five already.*

When Billie talks about her own marriage she talks as if she nearly married in the grave, whereas she was only thirty. But Mum was ashamed of being single for so long. How was it possible that her petite beauty had not attracted a husband? And in order to take the emphasis away from her own inability to find a partner, she blames Nanna Pearl for whimsically shifting house and state every couple of years while they grew up.

Nanna Pearl had no husband, beyond a few years, and therefore Billie and Bette have no father. Marrying Ted was like finding a father and husband in one. She took him inside her — made him part of her core. Her eyes go back to him when she's talking in a group and he is there. She has to touch him when they're in a crowd, and at night she always goes to bed when he does, even if she's not tired.

Ted describes himself as the concrete footings of the family, and uses adjectives like rock solid, stormproof and the all-weather family. We sound like Dulux paint, as if we can endure anything. The immovable and rather stagnant nature of these qualities makes me feel inert. I imagine a life with my parents stretching on and on.

Perhaps their troubles will stay the same, maybe worsen slightly but never recover. My mother will shrink with my father getting larger and larger inside her. I picture their refusal to see me getting stronger; the fogginess surrounding me getting thicker and my outline vanishing. I will waft off somewhere but never quite leave home or get it out of my system.

It is 1978. People with disabilities are still called handicapped or retarded. In our advertisements we proudly add that our shops have *air-conditioned comfort*. We call perms *cool waves*. We've only three television stations and my favourite show, even though I know I am too old for it, is 'Kimba the White Lion'. Our radio is still largely just AM stations, and Lionel Yorke is the grooviest DJ. The Elliotts have just bought a Sanyo (*That's Life*) colour TV and Dad says maybe we can get one next year (if the price comes down).

The daily newspaper costs twelve cents. Meat is advertised with the price per pound as well as the price per kilo, and the popular cuts include pocket steak and oyster blade. There's no Lotto, just the dollar lottery, and a bottle of Bacardi costs $7.50. Mum is going to buy those crimplene pull-on slacks from Irene Whyte's for $5.99. The Liberals are in power and there are two Democrats in the Senate. Stayfree are advertising beltless adhesive pads but they don't show them absorbing blue liquid on TV.

You can read astonished headlines in the *West Australian* like *'More US Blacks Win Office'*, while Toni Morrison wins the National Book Critics Circle Award for *Song of Solomon*. There is debate in the media about introducing late-night shopping, and vinyl-covered pouffes are all the rage. 'I Dream of Jeannie' is on TV in the afternoons, and the cartoon Footrot Flats replaces Gunsmoke in the paper. Cigarettes are still advertised and a packet of twenty-five du Mauriers will cost you eighty-six cents. Apartheid opponents are being shot dead in South Africa, while some Australians suggest we should have separate schools for white and Aboriginal children. Alan Bond is 1977 Australian of the Year. My mother loves the Dinah Shore show and thinks about learning Chinese cooking with Charles Wong at the Chinese Cooking School.

It's summer, and the last two weeks of January are set aside for the family holiday. We always go to Bunbury, with a rented caravan towed behind the family Holden station

wagon. We try to get the same spot in the park under a peeling paperbark tree, close to the amenities.

This summer will be a blur. Splotches of colour and
black and white. Clips like from an 8mm home movie.
Seeing myself. Some of it will be remembered and other bits
forgotten. I'll remember the feel of the ocean and the sting
of the salt in my eyes. I'll remember touching myself for the
first time. I'll remember the rhythm of Ben's breath match-
ing mine as he sleeps beside my bed. I'll forget Billie's face;
her eyes red and swollen from crying. I'll forget holding
Alison's hand while we watch the horizon as the sun falls
into the water.

When we're little Alison and I tan a deep brown. Mum
hasn't heard of sun-sense. Naked, our arms and legs are
tanned sticks radiating from fair-skinned bodies. The
Bunbury beach is for babies and old women who don't like
to get their hair wet. People bob in the water like unsinkable
foam buoys. The water is flat like one of Nanna Pearl's
pressed blue bed sheets.

For years we are content to build sandcastles and scoop
trenches with cupped fingers and graze our knees on coarse
yellow sand. Next we collect seashells and make bracelets
and play make-believe shipwrecks and desert islands. We
imagine our parents perish in whatever disaster the game
entails and are then free to live under pretend palm trees and
forage for forest food. Our lives become bliss. As teenagers
we lie on our towels reading books like *Watership Down*, and

concentrate on our tans. Finally we can't think of anything much worse than two weeks in Bunbury in a hired caravan with our parents.

Ted says that a caravanning holiday is his compromise to Billie. She refuses to camp. It's one thing Billie puts her foot down about. She says Ted has never taken her on a holiday where they've stayed in a motel or, God forbid, a hotel. Not even for her honeymoon. Mum would like to stay somewhere that has small lavender soaps wrapped in waxed paper on the edge of the basin and the bath. She'd like towels that smell of a large professional laundry. And she'd like to hang a Do Not Disturb sign over the outside doorknob. Billie says that if she ever agrees to camping, she's sure she'll never get to see the inside of a hotel room. For Billie, caravanning means she isn't so close to the ground and is slightly less likely to spend the day shifting sand with a pan and broom. For Dad, it's still a cheaper option.

Billie becomes increasingly fanatical cramped into a small aluminium box. She lays down groundsheets and tarpaulins and doormats, and is forever sweeping and cleaning and putting things right. She says it's the confines of the place that insist on a certain order and fastidiousness. *Otherwise the sand just takes over*, she says. *Hose yourselves down before you come anywhere near this caravan*, she says. *Shoes off or else. Don't bring that sand in here with you or you won't hear the last of it.*

Imagining someone like Billie in a caravan park isn't

easy. She's at odds with the place. She hasn't got that down-to-earth approach you see in caravan parks. She doesn't like to be overheard. She doesn't like people to know she has bowels. She doesn't like to just chat. She isn't comfortable standing next to a stranger in a communal bathroom while she brushes her teeth with her homemade paste of bicarb and a drop of peppermint oil.

Ted says he and Billie can go round the country in a caravan in a few years, like it would be her dream come true. He says, *You shouldn't waste money on silly things like a bed for the night when you can sleep under the stars.* But I don't think he has a lot of money; not the kind of money you need for hotels. After all, he cuts lawns for a living and refuses to let his wife work. Mum says it's probably our last proper holiday as a family, since Alison will be turning seventeen next year and then who knows where she'll be. Alison has been saying she's going to university. She wants to study politics at the ANU in Canberra, but nobody takes her seriously. Billie says we should do something different so we'll all remember this summer as a special holiday.

Ted snorts. He says, *We are not going to a hotel.* He says Billie is being hysterical — his favourite word to describe her. He says he wishes she would just get over this *time* and return to normal. I don't know what normal he means. He looks down at her and the only noise is the sound of air leaving his nostrils. It's a louder sound than exhalation, as if he's forcing the air out. Like he has an insect up his nose.

He won't speak to her for days. When she addresses him he turns away, gets up and walks out of the room. The house seems stiff when they argue or, more precisely, when they stop speaking. The silence takes on a sound of its own and my head feels as if it might implode with the pressure. The television volume is turned up and the only voices are the game show hosts and the newsreaders. I wish the ABC newsman was my dad; he has smiley eyes.

Dad stops touching as well. He's forever grabbing Billie and holding her about the waist. They touch one another a lot. In the evenings they sit on the couch together and she puts her legs on him. When they fight they sit in separate chairs, with their backs straight and their eyes on the television. I am not sure how they make up. It just goes back to normal after a few days.

Dad says he's off to get the caravan. Mum's mouth looks small and tight like a baby bird's. When we hear the car pull up, an hour or so later, she goes into their bedroom and slams the door. Alison and I want to see it, hoping this one might be more modern than the last. We want to see what new features it has and remind ourselves of the dinky, toy-like fridge and pump-action tap. There's a certain excitement about the arrival of a caravan that even teenagers feel.

The empty tow ball shines up at us and Ted steps out of the car dangling a set of keys from his large hand. Billie is at the bedroom window. Her face looks small, peering out between the curtains. She comes outside. He says, *Darl, you'll never guess what I've got planned. A cottage. Everything provided and right by the beach.* He opens up his arms like he expects all three of us to run towards him and hurl ourselves at him. Billie does just that.

Ted has decided we are going to spend the two weeks in a shack at Singleton beach, not even as far away as Mandurah. He lets Mum think it is in deference to her. Alison says it is his idea, and has nothing to do with Billie not wanting another caravanning holiday.

Billie and Ted stand there hugging. My body sags seeing them in one another's arms. I want to be part of that hug but instead I stand there and watch. Alison turns away and walks off. I wonder what she does this for. Isn't she happy that they are hugging? Isn't this a good thing? Am I missing something that she knows? After all, she is my source of wisdom about these things.

She is the one who gives me the answers about our parents' marriage. When I tell her I'm frightened that they don't love one another and will get a divorce, she shrugs her shoulders and shakes her head. She says it won't happen. *Not a chance in hell.* Like she'd enjoy it if they did. Like it would be a spectacle in an otherwise dull life. *The fights are just like the rumblings of a volcano. Those things only erupt every thousand years or so.* She says people like Billie and Ted are made for one another. It's as if she can view the marriage and our family from outside, a few feet away, a detached observer. I am concealed inside it.

When my mother pulls out of the hug I see that she was crying. My shoulders loosen, my stomach untwists. Ted puffs himself out and his chest expands and fills his shirt as he says, *Everything for my girls.* He hasn't noticed Alison's withdrawal.

Billie is a small woman. When she was younger and we were babies people would look at her and Ted and say, *It must have been difficult having those children, the father being such a big man and all.* A big man and a small woman often have people wondering. She likes to tell us how we had to be delivered by Caesarean, or else we would have remained inside her. I imagine growing old within her, squashed against her ribs, the crease of her spine against the side of my face, unable to straighten and stretch. A woman trapped inside the womb of her mother.

Billie wants to be on people's minds. She is conscious of them looking at her, as if her eyes and ears have trained in on people observing her. Her eyes constantly dart and blink. She watches her reflection as she passes shop windows and adjusts the side mirror so that she can see herself when she's in the car. She likes that people look at Ted and say, *What a big strong man your husband is.* Her smallness only accentuates Ted's gargantuan frame. Gentleness is implied by his size. The concept of the gentle giant follows Ted around.

Billie has immaculate hair and nails. She believes people notice things like fingernails and good shoes. Because she judges people by such things, she thinks everybody does. She never lets her shoes look scuffed and favours a two-inch heel. Billie is her appearance; a veneer of calm, stiff sprayed hair that doesn't move even in a howling easterly pulled back and clumped high on the back of her head, a powdered face, orange or pink lipstick (red is too common) and shoes that cover your toes. *Only babies have sweet toes*, she says.

I remember my mother as the epitome of womanhood. I am half her size; podgy, but still doll-like. I look up at her and see her breasts are perfectly pointed cones and her stomach is flat and firm. I don't know she wears a girdle and harnesses her bosom in a cross-your-heart brassiere. She is as unreal as a shop mannequin. As a little girl I can never quite imagine being like her. She has a grown-upness that I cannot envisage attaining.

I gave up long ago. I know I will never be the manicured type. My strain of boyishness that so irritated Billie is an immovable stain. No amount of combing and straightening could tip me into Billie's realm. As a teenager I wear too much brown or have a scab on my knee. Not to mention the chewed fingernails and the need to twirl and twist strands of hair that fall around my face.

When we are little Billie is the kind of woman you don't want to hug for fear of crushing her. Not because she is small, but because she is so well ironed. The air is tense

17

around her — an invisible barrier that wards off would-be embracers. Her starchiness is a signal to peck her on the cheek. Barely parted lips brush the floury surface, her head gently angled away. Or else she presents both her hands for you to hold.

It is 1999. The media uses politically correct language, but racism and sexism are just better disguised. A footballer pays a self-imposed $20,000 fine to an Aboriginal charity for calling another player *a black cunt*. Feminism is supposed to have liberated women, but in the West we are still paid less than men and the poorest people in the world are female. We have five television stations and cable if we want, and the Internet and email. We can shop without cash and pay all our bills over the phone. We've all got colour televisions and one in the bedroom. People don't buy the newspaper like they used to. Everything is metric except when we think of the weight of babies, and people buy organic meat and barn-laid eggs and new-fashioned pork; anything with a red tick from the Heart Foundation. Fresh pasta and Turkish bread and chemical-free chicken. People are on Naltrexone, Prozac or Viagra. Everyone has a Lotto dream and winning the Powerball could net you fifteen million.

Olympics signify corruption and scandal. Some people are worried about the millennium bug and surviving Y2K.

The Liberals are in power. The world watches war on television while NATO bombs Serbia and the ethnic Albanians are driven from their homes in Kosovo. The media calls it ethnic cleansing, and killing civilians is collateral damage. On TV sanitary napkins are super absorbent and wafer thin and soak up gallons of blue liquid or anything else you spill on the floor. Toni Morrison is known of in Australia and Oprah Winfrey makes *Beloved* into a dismal vehicle of her own. 'I Dream of Jeannie' is still on TV in the afternoons and my favourite shows are 'ER' and 'Animal Hospital'. Cigarettes are expensive and never advertised, and you are not supposed to smoke anyway. The government has a war on drugs and zero tolerance is a popular concept. South Africa is rid of apartheid and East Timor gets a bloodied independence. Alan Bond is in prison and paints pictures. Billie watches Ricki Lake and 'Australia's Most Wanted', and thinks about learning Italian.

Billie's sheen has faded even though she still attempts a facade. The years of believing herself to be diseased have imprinted lines across her forehead. Lumbago, sciatica, endometriosis, sinusitis, migraine headaches, bronchitis, glomerulonephritis, hypertension and colitis. She wears thick alabaster-coloured foundation and powders her face as if she's dusting fairy cakes with icing sugar. Her skin is crumpled like discarded pink tissue paper. I wonder if her small blue eyes see her reflection as though the mirror is smeared with Vaseline. I think she doesn't see the deep creases her face has acquired. She thinks putting on her face is a sign she is living. She says that women who don't wear make-up don't pay enough attention to how they present themselves to the world. She says, *Do they believe people don't notice?*

Mostly she has given up with me. She sees my plain unmade-up face and I know it bothers her. Her eyes squint slightly as she peers at me and she asks if I want to *borrow a bit of colour*. Sometimes she grabs my hand before I've realised it's my nails she wants to inspect, and she *tut tuts* her tongue on the roof of her mouth.

Now when I hug her I still feel a slight reticence on her part, as if she'd prefer to greet me with an extended hand. But I fold my arms around her all the same. I have my father's large frame and, besides, she is shrinking. I feel how unsubstantial she is. At my shoulder I see the permed hair hiding her pale scalp. I lean my cheek over and let it touch her hair. It's soft and springy and smells of perming solution. Metallic. When I release her I watch her walk down the hall and from behind can imagine she is someone else's mother. She can't maintain the posture she was so proud of and her once petite and delicate steps are now a shuffle.

In 1978 Billie is forty-eight years old. She is menopausal but I don't know this. I think we, her teenage children, trigger her irritability. I think her snapping at us is our fault. Sometimes I think she is jealous of our youth, and of Alison's more than mine. Alison looks like a woman now. She is slender like a young sapling gum. Her arms hang down and she fingers the edge of her short skirt. Her thighs are a smooth brown like water-polished river rock. Her long tawny legs are the envy of small women like our mother.

Alison has matured in the way I think women are supposed to mature. Certainly it is how Billie expects, and it's a way I already sense will not be mine. Her hips have broadened, but not too much; she has grown taller and developed B cup breasts. Not awkward wads of flesh in all the wrong places. No rolls over her hip bones or fatty bosoms like plump cushions. She reminds me of Marcia Brady. She does the same thing with her mouth that Marcia has perfected — a smile and pout in one.

Lately my presence seems to annoy Alison. She shuts her door all the time as if she has something to hide, and asks me to knock before I come in. She calls what I do *barging*. She says I don't have any respect for people's privacy, but I can't see what she would want to keep from me. There isn't a thing I would hide from her. I want her to know everything about me so she can help me sort through it. Sometimes I wish I could have her like a little person inside my head and she could sweep it all out. Shuffle the stuff inside around and throw out all the garbage. I think she would know what to keep and what to bin.

But it isn't like it used to be between us when we were small. We don't sit on the sofa so close that the hairs on our forearms touch each other. She pushes me away and says, *This far.* Her arm is outstretched as she measures the distance between us. *This is how far from someone you should sit,* she says. *Not on top.* She says she is telling me for my own good. She says she wants me to learn how to get on with people. *No one else will care to teach you,* she says.

Mum picks us up from the local pool for a visit to her doctor. She toots the car horn and we see her hand beckoning us from the window. I imagine her foot pumping the accelerator as she waits, and her putting out her cigarette, since she knows I say it makes me carsick.

At Dr Urqhart's rooms in an old federation house in Cottesloe we wait with our mother for the appointment. The other patients speak in hushed voices as if they're in church, while Billie complains, in an overly loud voice, of hot flushes. She embarrasses us by cooling herself with an oriental fan as we sit in the cool rosewood waiting room. She says she has a constant ringing in her ears as if a blowfly is trapped inside her ear canal and is beating its wings on her eardrum. I contemplate her condition and wonder if she is going mad, like Lady Macbeth.

Mum says she thinks it's the change of life. Alison seems to know what she means. Billie tells Alison she wants to ask Doctor what effect it will have on her skin elasticity. Already she feels it sagging in all the wrong places. She arches her neck and shows us the perfect wrinkle-free skin over her throat. *I don't want to lose this,* she says, rubbing her fingertips over her smooth brown skin.

I don't know what the change of life is. I think Billie must be having some psychological crisis. I haven't started menstruating yet and can barely imagine it beginning, let alone it ending some thirty-five years later.

Billie asks the nurse how long Doctor will be. He is running behind and Billie wants to be home before Ted. She wants Alison weighed because she thinks she is too thin and me weighed because she thinks I'm too heavy. *It could be just dense bones, like your father,* she says, *but we'd better be sure.* She says I should be over the puppy-fat stage.

The waiting room smells of methylated spirits. The vinyl-covered seats are squeaking under my sweaty thighs. Mum thumbs through a *Woman's Day* till the doctor pokes his head round the heavy door to his office and signals us in with a tilt of his head. I feel a nervous wave of butterflies in my stomach as he looks over his glasses at us and I recall past probing.

Mum recounts her concerns and he tells us to take our dresses off and stand in our underpants and singlets for him to see. Alison is wearing a soft cotton bra with little bluebells on it while I am embarrassed by my spongy breasts under my Bonds singlet. He pinches the skin around my waist with his cold smooth fingers and nods slowly. He asks Alison to put her arms above her head and runs his hand down the side of her rib cage and nods again. He takes the glass lid off the jellybean container on his desk and asks if we're too old for sweeties. We take one each, even though I wonder if he's testing me with this offer.

Alison steps on the scales first and the red pointer swings to just under seven stone. I see the way her hip bones push at her skin like those of a half-starved horse. *Mmm,* says Doctor, as he notes the weight down on his pad with an elegant fountain pen. The pen scratches the paper. My turn. I tread on gently but still the pointer arcs and swings rapidly to the right as if it will hit the far end and not stop. I don't want to put my other foot down. It hovers just above the other. The doctor taps my leg with his pen as if he knows what I'm doing. They all stare at the scales. I look at my feet as they seem to flatten and spread over the black rubber surface. I don't look at the numbers.

We get back in our clothes and are told to wait outside for Mum, since she has her own questions. She is in there for ages and we wonder what he will tell her about us.

Mum says the doctor agreed with her about our weights and that Alison is to put on weight or risk being infertile (she has to eat more than Ryvitas and hard green apples) and I need to slim down or I will never find a husband. Not just heavy bones, it seems. Alison is more able to ignore Billie than I, even though having a husband isn't something I have spent much time thinking about. I'm not sure that I will want one.

Billie says the doctor helped her with her change of life (that phrase again), and he says there's no harm in the old remedies her mother used — it may even delay some of the skin ageing. She says she's going to take a cold friction bath every morning and full warm baths two or three times a week. The cold bath is supposed to keep the skin active and equalise the circulation of blood to help prevent the oppressive hot flushes. Mum is a great believer in baths. She got the idea from Nanna Pearl, who inflicted baths of various temperatures on young Billie and Bette as well as herself. If the baths don't help then she will try the hormone the doctor has suggested.

Nanna Pearl grew up in the era of baths, when there was a bath remedy for everything. Her favourite was a cold sitz bath where the bather sat in a tub of cold water rubbing her hips and thighs while her feet remained in a basin of piping hot water. This bath was used for congestion of the womb and pelvic organs. Cold plunge baths were for strengthening the constitution, whereas a tepid bath was good for the nerves. Then there was the hot footbath with a few teaspoons of mustard added to the water for congestion of the brain. It was important to get the temperature just right, so you had to have a bath thermometer and an endless supply of boiling kettles. The water started at 105°F and was increased gradually to 120°F, and at the end of the bath the feet received a dash of cold water and were then dried vigorously. (The old sitz bath is now a rusty planter for a herb garden near the blue-painted back door of Nanna Pearl's.)

Nanna Pearl believes that your feet should be kept warm and dry, and that cold feet, especially when menstruating, can cause serious inflammation of the womb. I tell Nanna Pearl that I haven't started my periods yet and she says she hopes it's not a bad omen. *Baths in general,* she says, *keep the skin active and therefore help the kidneys.* I think congestion was a big problem in her day.

1998. A year ago. Billie's white enamel claw-foot bath has a green stain where the tap drips. Above it, on the pale yellow wall, is a laminated diagram of breast self-examination. I think about Billie standing in the bath under the shower rose, one elbow raised and her other hand over her small sunken bosom, searching for lumps. Her fingers probe the edges of a benign bump while she imagines a cancerous spreading mass.

The bath's feet have wedged themselves into the linoleum, like the footprints of a dog on wet sand. There is a soggy towel underneath it, collecting water that leaks from the rusted plughole. But it is still a beautiful bath; deep and solid and a reminder to me of when Alison and I shared it as children.

We are small enough to stretch our arms and legs out and slide under the water. We hold our breath and see who can stay submerged the longest. We wring out flannels into our mouths and then squirt out a spray of water like a little boy pissing. We lie with flannels over our faces and suck them to our skin as if they are jellyfish. We play for hours with a cup and a teapot, letting out the lukewarm water and rerunning the hot tap till Billie hears the igniting sound of the gas flame and bangs on the kitchen wall to signal *enough wasting gas.*

I am cleaning her tub because it's hard for her to bend over and really scrub it. The Jif is lifting the smudges and tea-like stains from inside the bath. The room is unchanged and the avocado-coloured sink looks small and childlike. My hands are enormous around the chrome taps. Man hands. I clean the streaks of toothpaste from the old mirror. Pasted beside it is a magazine clipping showing different types of moles. The paper's edge is frayed and yellow. The images are of magnified nipples and ear lobes obscured by darkly pigmented skin. It says, *The ABCD of skin cancer. Asymmetry. Border irregularity. Colour. Diameter.* I picture Billie at the mirror, her fingertips tracing the circumference of minute and harmless moles, reading her body's Braille.

I look at the one pink toothbrush alone in its rack made for a family of four. I remember Ted's brush; the way its bristles were always angled and worn more than anyone else's because he scrubbed too hard. I have to bend my head to look in the mirror, when once I could barely see the top of my hair. In the reflection I see Billie's floral shower cap hanging behind me on the back of the door, its daisy centres like black eyes watching me work, and next to her cap a man's unused dressing gown.

Billie comes in while I'm cleaning and says I'm doing a good job. She says she can't wait to get in there and have a good soak. Epsom salts. She says her old bones are feeling their age and sometimes she worries about slipping and falling and breaking a hip like Mrs M from over the road. *It just snapped like dry kindling,* she says. I suggest handrails, but I know she is only telling me of her frailty because she thinks otherwise I will not come to visit and check on her. Why, when I come every week and sometimes twice or three times, does she think I will suddenly stop coming? I don't know why I have yet to convince her of my loyalty.

She says she is dying, or rather fading away. She doesn't use the word dying, as if it's bad manners. She's been dying for so long that I wonder whether, when she finally does die, it will come as much of a shock. Perhaps I will find her asleep in the bath, her small body pale and prune-like, her head resting back against the rim of the tub, a few strands of wet hair curled on her neck, her last thought that of Ted.

When we get back from our visit to the doctor's, Dad is at home writing a list of things we will need to take with us on our holiday. His large fingers look clumsy and unfamiliar around a pen and I think it is the only time, other than his invoices for the lawn-mowing, that I've seen him write. His spelling is bad and Alison makes fun of the list where he misspells common household items — tiolet paper, suger, fluor and bred. I laugh too, but inside I feel sad for him as I see a nerve in his face twitch. He gives the list to Alison and says for *smarty pants* to finish it. Billie says we should show more respect; after all, *Dad is taking us on a special holiday this year that is costing an arm and a leg.*

Dad works hard to support us and he tells people he has paid off the house and has a wife who doesn't need to work. Billie and Ted's roles are strictly separate, and for Ted it would be unthinkable for Billie to have a job, even though she's offered to go back to hairdressing several times when Dad has said business is slow or things are a bit tight.

It's hard to imagine Mum as a working woman. Aunt Bette says she was one of those hairdressers that made you think she knew what would best suit your face. She would ignore any of your suggestions and cut your hair the way she thought would complement your most attractive features. She'd say things like, *This haircut will take the emphasis away from your nose.* Of course it didn't please everyone and she upset a few clients with her bossiness. I can't picture her being in control like that. Nanna Pearl made her a tapestry-covered footstool that she would stand on to get a height advantage while cutting the top of someone's hair.

Ted has built up a busy mowing business in the lawn-proud suburbs around where we live. He has a mower with a roller that he says just glides along. It doesn't pull at the lawn, but cuts and presses it. He scrupulously maintains the blades and the motor, never pushing it when it doesn't want to cut; turning it off to go over paths and driveways; picking up sticks and clothes pegs rather than mowing through them. He harps on about respecting your tools. He sweeps up after himself and trims the edges. The owners pass on his name from house to house, so sometimes he does three or four gardens in the one street. He calls himself a landscape gardener.

For as long as I can remember Alison and I go with him during school holidays. Is it to give Mum a break or is it to help Dad? We aren't sure which. We don't mind going unless it's a stinker. We are given our jobs to do, usually raking and sweeping or sometimes pulling weeds while the lawn mower drones on around the back. We like being at other people's places seeing their things, and maybe if they have a pool we will be allowed to use it. The housewives love us. They praise Dad's *gorgeous daughters* (I think they're referring to Alison) and say, *Such good girls to be helping your father*, as if we had a choice.

There is no choice, at least not for me. In the summer of 1978 it seems Mum wants to be on her own, and she asks Dad to take us most days.

It's a boiling day. It is hot before the sun is up. It will be the third day of over 35-degree heat. Alison and I want to stay home and lie around on the cool carpet in the darkened house, watch TV and make popcorn. In the early morning

Mum goes round the house closing all the windows, open to the fresh night air. She lowers the bamboo blinds so the light is fractured and dim. The house stays cool and she marvels at the stationary mercury in the thermometer on the mantel-piece as the temperature outside rises. Maybe Alison will play Monopoly with me, the Christmas present from Aunt Bette. The cool floor on our stomachs. But Billie says she has the house to clean and doesn't want us under her feet. We ask why she is cleaning when we are going on holidays in a couple of days. She says she wants it to be spick and span when we return. We say we could help her if she wants, but she says, *Take 'em please, Darl.*

Alison is quick to remember a reason she can't come. She has to go shopping in Claremont with a friend for the friend's sister's wedding. It is complicated and very impor-tant and she almost forgot. I can't find a reason not to go.

It is just Ted and me along the bench seat of the ute. When Alison is with us I have to sit in the middle since I'm the youngest, even though I'm bigger width-wise. My body wedges between them and I'm concious of my heavy thighs next to her thin legs. It's often hot and breathless in the front, and while Ted and Alison have the advantage of the open windows I get no air in the middle. Usually there's bird poo right in my line of vision. But today there is an expanse of empty seat between Ted and me. I think my legs look slimmer with so much room to myself. I put my face half-out of the open window and imagine I am a dog with its happy head in the breeze, my hair its flapping ears. I make barking noises at passing cars. Dad drives one-handed with his right arm out the window, tapping the side of the ute.

The sun is just up and there's a yellow light across the lawns. People have their sprinklers on. There are sprinklers, like tiny tractors, that move by themselves along the line of the hose. We start at Mrs Johns' in Kinninmont Street, because she is always up early and her neighbours have never complained to her about being woken by the lawn-mowing. Dad thinks people should understand that he needs to start early in this heat, but still he has to pick where he starts to avoid disturbing people who sleep late.

To Dad, sleeping late is almost as bad as being over-weight. He says you miss the best part of the day if you miss the dawn. He thinks that to lie in bed shows a lack of moti-vation and severe laziness. In the mornings, when he is up, everyone knows about it. The radio goes on and he bangs around in the kitchen making tea. On summer mornings he walks around naked. Alison and I tell him we think it's gross, but he says the body is beautiful and natural and nothing to be ashamed of (as long as it's looked after). He knows it embarrasses us. Once Ted finds something that irritates you, he enjoys doing it all the more. I don't remem-ber noticing his nakedness when I was small, but at fourteen anybody's nakedness is a fright. We keep our heads in our cereal bowls and try to avoid looking at his pendulous bits. Billie's dressing gown, in contrast, seems to get more and more constrictive as she wraps the cotton tightly about her and clasps it to her neck. She doesn't say anything to him about his nudity.

Mrs Johns overwaters her buffalo grass, says Ted as he takes the mower off the back of the ute. *See how spongy it is?* The grass is thick and a dark green. She has two oval rose gardens in the front that are full of apricot-coloured roses, and she asks Ted to mulch around them with the grass clippings. She's fussy about her edges. As I sweep the red cement path, I notice the way my flesh wobbles on my thighs when I move. Not thinner after all.

By nine o'clock we have done three lawns and it is over thirty. My knees are dirty and my arms are sunburnt and stinging. Ted works without a shirt in the summer and is a red-brick brown. He doesn't burn. He thinks that the skin gets used to the sun and that his tan is a sign of good health. When he sees a pale person he says, *Look at that pasty face.*

We are at Mrs Teasdale's, our fourth house in Kinninmont Street, and have finished her lawn and edges. Dad has wheeled the mower up the grey planks onto the back of the ute and is folding the tarpaulin for collecting the grass clippings. He says he has to go inside and talk to Mrs Teasdale about her landscaping plans. He says she has a big project for him to do after our holiday. He tells me I can listen to the radio in the car. But the car is like an oven and I can't stay in there long. I sit in the shade of the hedge facing the house. I feel the sharp cut ends of the freshly mown lawn under my thighs. A ladybird lands on my leg and I hold it in my closed hand. I feel its legs tickle my skin as it wanders my palm. I take it to a rose bush so it can eat the aphids. A thin stem with a fading rose, the edges of its petals burnt and dry, is so weighted down with the small green insects that it bends towards the earth. A thorny stem hooks my top and holds me. I am stuck in the rose garden, surrounded by the lemon and tea scent. As I untangle my shirt I see a movement at the window. A woman's pale milky hand tilts the venetians. Her fingers fidget at the corner of the blind and I know the room at the front of the house is not the kitchen. I have been in the kitchen before. I know that room is the bedroom and I think that Mrs Teasdale is in there with Ted. I watch for the smallest disturbance of the blind till I feel the urge to urinate.

I find the old toilet round the back under the grapevine, behind a fruit tree abuzz with flies. There are cobwebs, thick and grey, arcing the corners of the dunny door. Brown leaves and bits of bark litter the floor. I perch above the toilet seat and wee. Its trickle sounds loud on the dull, dry porcelain and I realise there is no button to push or chain to pull. No paper. I jump a few times to let the drops fall and then pull up my pants.

I fall asleep under the shade of an old gum and when I wake up there is a thin trickle of dried saliva crossing my chin like a snail trail on a footpath. The shapes of the shade have changed and my legs are in the sun. I get up and search for more ladybirds. Dad takes the longest time.

We are in the car going to the next lawn. I look at Ted and watch his profile. I see an old scar near his eye from when an aberrant stick flew up and hit him in the face after being mown over. He sings along with the radio, out of tune. He smells of soap. He smells clean and sweat-free when normally he smells of grass and petrol, earth and salt.

After one more lawn he smells again of freshly cut grass and I can convince myself the other scent was imagined. I say to Ted, *I think Mrs Teasdale could do with some sun,* but instead of agreeing and making some comment on her sickly paleness he says, *Women should look after their skin — it's more sensitive.*

1982. I am turning nineteen and living with Billie. We share the family home as if we are the eighty-year-old sisters across the road. Large bushes cling to the house and the weeds have grown tall in the garden beds. The rose bushes have a disease and the dark green leaves have turned yellow. White lacy bugs inhabit the potato vine. I imagine their mouths chomping through the vegetation till we are left with nothing but dry stalks. Dead leaves drop on the clean washing. I have plans to straighten it up but Billie thinks I should leave it. She says, *What's the point of a lovely garden?*

I have been working in a vet clinic as a kennel girl for nearly a year. I am beginning to feel comfortable in the company of the other staff, not just the animals. I spend less time in the back kennels and help out more in the hospital part, answer the phone when the others are too busy, and even serve customers out the front. My large palms sweat on the money as I hand them their change.

The others used to stop talking when I entered the staff room. They would go quiet and look into their cups, or else say they had to get on with a surgery or X-ray and leave me alone in the room. I felt like I shouldn't be there, like I should eat my lunch in the kennels, and often I did, the three-legged marmalade kennel cat on my lap. Now they keep talking and sometimes ask me what I've done on the weekend. Paul, the young graduate vet, is talking about his sex life. He says that women who swallow during oral sex develop antibodies against sperm and this can be contraceptive. The two nurses laugh loudly and I can see Clare's fillings in her back teeth. They don't cover their mouths when they laugh like Billie says you should. Paul says they should try it sometime. He says his girlfriend told him it tasted like orange juice. *Full of vitamins.* Clare says, *That's obscene.*

What do you think, Cat? Paul says to me. I think about cocktail sausages and frankfurters dipped in Heinz tomato sauce, icy poles and toothache. I turn away to fill up the kettle and reach into the cupboard for a clean mug. *Would you like a coffee?* I say in reply. I wonder if I'm the only woman in the place that hasn't tasted a man's semen.

I go back to the cool kennels with my cup of coffee and sit on the still-damp concrete, wet from antiseptic and hosing. I watch a dog through the kennel mesh as it sleeps with its head on its paws and see its eyes twitch while it dreams. It's a dog without a home and the boss says it will have to be euthanased. I put my fingers through the mesh and touch its nose, the soft velvet part above its black button, and its eyes slowly open. I think about its death and work myself up over it. It's like I do it on purpose. Like I want to cry about something but don't know what, so I cry about the black kelpie cross with no name. I open the kennel door and he comes into my lap like he is consoling me. He licks my face. I tell him he's going to die and I should be comforting him, not the other way around. But his nature is to please me. I think about his sincerity; how good it is that he can't speak and ruin everything with dirty silly words. His communication is simple and clean and true.

The washing machine finishes a load of dog blankets and I take them out of the machine and load them into a laundry basket. Even washed they retain that earthy smell of dog shit. I don't mind it like other people. I take the basket out to the Hills Hoist in the concrete yard and begin to hang them out. I peg them neatly around the hoist, using the pegs sparingly since there are never enough. Corner to corner. I feel the afternoon sun searing my uncovered shoulders. Clare comes out with a load of surgical drapes and asks me to hang them out, and when I've finished she's got some instruments for me to clean inside. I think how she's supposed to hang out the hospital washing, but I don't say anything, just wonder if I'll have enough pegs for it all. I decide to hang hers first since it doesn't matter if mine blow off.

As I walk around the hoist I see Paul sitting on the staff room steps. He has a cigarette dangling between his fingers, held near his feet. I've never seen him smoke before. His head is down and one hand rubs his forehead, his elbow supported by his knee. I see his socks are unmatching and think he must not live at home. I imagine trying to get out the door without Billie noticing clashing socks and making me change them. Sometimes I think she believes a kennel girl is someone who people notice.

I have several pegs jutting out of my mouth when I see Paul and I remember his semen comment. Immediately my neck goes hot and blotchy. I spit the pegs out onto the concrete and he looks up at the noise. He strolls over as if to talk to me and then stands against the fence as I bend and pick the pegs up, putting them in a pile on top of the laundry. He watches the laundry basket as he speaks.

I just killed a dog, he says. I put the washing down and ask him what happened. He says he doesn't know. He says he anaesthetised it and it just dropped off the needle, like euthanasia except it was supposed to be a teeth clean. *It was only four years old — a sweet Lhaso Apso. It just stopped breathing when it shouldn't have and then there was no heartbeat and we couldn't revive it. It's my first death like that,* he says. I see moisture in his eyes, but instead of crying he thumps the fence with his fist and then cradles his hand as if it's stung. *Do the owners know?* I ask. *No, I've tried ringing, no one's home*, he says and then says, *fuck fuck fuck*. I don't know what to say and so I start hanging out the washing again. I absent-mindedly load my mouth with pegs. *Thanks,* he says. He stubs his cigarette out and goes back inside.

1998. Billie is sixty-eight and several inches shorter than I am when we go walking down the cool verdant streets. Her doctor says she should walk every day and so I take her out around a few blocks when I visit. Sometimes she still goes on her own. We see a middle-aged woman with a sparkling gold sun visor walking a small poodle on a retractable lead. She's power walking. *Notice how those lycra shorts give her no control,* says Billie, commenting on the woman's protruding belly. The blue-coated dog stops to defecate and gold visor walks to the end of the lead's extension before she feels the resistance of the little dog in the middle of its business. She walks on the spot while it finishes, her knees lifting high as she maintains her exercise. I remember the way Ben tugged on his lead, straining on his choker till he gagged when he picked up the smell of another dog on his route; lifting his leg on anything vertical and leaving his scent.

Billie stops outside a familiar house and rests her hand on a rambling plumbago hedge. It's covered in small blue flowers and needs trimming. I watch her hand pluck the tiny flowers and mince the petals between her fingers. She says she thinks Ted had affairs. She says that even though a part of her was sure of his infidelities, she didn't entirely believe her own instinct. She says she sent us with him on his rounds because she thought our presence would curtail him. During the school holidays she felt safe and secure that he would not be servicing more than their lawns. Her voice is caustic and thin as she recalls her anxiousness. She thought he wouldn't risk being found out by his daughters. She says she thought one of us would tell her if we suspected or witnessed an indiscretion.

Since there was not a peep from us, she made herself believe she was being paranoid. She believed she was consumed by her own jealousy. Sometimes it was so large and overwhelming inside her that she hurt herself so as to escape it. She took a razor blade to the inside of her thighs and cut thin wobbly lines a few inches long. When she saw the blood and felt the sharp stinging cut, she felt better. She would cry and run her finger along the shallow wound. She tasted her blood on her fingers.

I ask this small bent woman beside me why she thought her husband, my father, was unfaithful. She looks up at me, as if she is the child and I am the mother. She takes my hand in hers and I feel how delicate and impractical it is. Her skin has aged and the colour is uneven, like the motley bark of a plane tree. But her nails are impeccable; manicured and painted a coral pink. She says she saw him with a woman one day, walking down Hampden Road, and she followed behind them for a short while. She thought their bodies moved too close to one another for client and gardener; that they walked too slowly, as only people in love do. When she questioned Ted about the woman he said they'd gone out to discuss her garden plans over coffee since she was having her house fumigated that day.

So I tell her about my memory. I tell her of Ted smelling like pink Lux, of his singing out of tune to the radio. I tell her I saw the woman's hand at the window and how I thought the window belonged to a bedroom.

Yes, that was Mrs Teasdale. This is the house, she says. The name is familiar. I look at the old house, its orange roof tiles overgrown with grey-green lichen, and remember the lawn under my legs and the wan hand at the window. A large hibiscus with heavy pink flowers obscures the glass. Billie tells me how Mrs Teasdale came to Ted's memorial service and cried. Billie saw her hold a white hanky to her eyes. It was as if the hanky magnified itself in her vision. She says she knew then that she had been right about the affair. The part of her that couldn't believe Ted was dead walked past Mrs Teasdale's house every day for three years in case she caught a glimpse of Ted there, having set up house with his mistress, despite the presence of a freckled Mr Teasdale. Eventually the house was sold and the Teasdales moved on. When she saw the For Sale sign she found a new walking route.

I ask her if she ever spoke to Mrs Teasdale about Ted, and she tells me how one day she was walking past the house, her head raised high to see over the hedge, when Mrs Teasdale stood up from her gardening. They stood facing one another. Billie says Mrs Teasdale's eyes were such a light blue and her skin so pale that she seemed translucent. Like a pearl. The woman extended her hand across the hedge towards her and Billie thinks she was about to say something when instead Billie turned and walked away. She says the clip-clop of her shoes on the pavement sounded so loud that she left the path and walked on the grass verge. She says she felt Mrs Teasdale watching her and she tried to keep her back straight and her steps even, her arms by her sides. She says her heels stuck in the thick lawn and she felt herself stumble. All she could think was how clumsy and unlady-like she must look from behind. Suddenly she was struck by the ridiculousness of high heels. After that she gave up wearing the two-inch heels she'd worn all her married life.

Five years ago. I am thirty. I move out of home. It is diffi-cult to do, but I know that the part of me that says Billie needs me is the part that lies to make myself feel better. The thought of being in the house when she dies is too much.

I move into a share house with two girls I hardly know. Joelle and Pippa. We have only just met.

I first meet Joelle at the vet clinic. She is a final-year school student doing work experience and talking about moving out of home. She is fighting with her father. She says he hates her. He threw her against a glass door in an argument and she burst right through it. She has a scar like a lightning bolt on her forearm from a shard of fractured glass. I think she is brazen and cocky. She reminds me of Alison when she was seventeen and leaving home, Billie and me.

At the end of the week of work experience she says she's found a place for herself and her friend Pippa, but they need another person, and would I be interested. I'm surprised she's asked me since we've only known each other four days. *Why me?* I ask. She says that she thinks I will be a stabilising influence for them, and that I'm motherly — or rather, a bit of an old chook. Besides, she likes the way I have these strange little dogs. She and Pippa want to help look after them.

At thirty I'm a straight single inexperienced virginal conscientious pale pink sombre sorrowful would-be vegetarian conservative honest clean blemished fussy obsessive animal lover. I'm moving into a house with two seventeen-year-olds who are smart sexy bisexual nice-girls experienced radical messy orgasmic vegetarian pierced garrulous musical wounded caring feminist animal lovers.

I think it's strange they want someone who wears calico pants and baggy cotton shirts to share their house. Someone big. I feel reckless, like anything might happen. I think they have the wrong impression of me. But I stop trying to analyse *why me*. I say yes. I think the way they are might rub off on me.

But I don't move in straightaway. It takes me a few months to unravel myself from Billie. I help them out with the rent and sign the lease and they say they'll keep my room vacant till I can get away. They say they know what a drag parents can be. Joelle calls in at work once a week and asks if I'm moving in sometime soon. They have a friend staying in my room. Just for a few days.

Billie is sixty-four and we have lived together, just the two of us, for nearly sixteen years. When the day comes for me to move out, Billie has inexplicable cramps in her stomach. She crawls along the Berber carpet to my room, where I'm packing a suitcase, and pokes her head around the door. She has a fist in her belly and her head down. She lifts her head, opens her mouth and howls. I help her to her feet and sit her down on my bed. Her face is white and I wonder if she could be bleeding internally.

I drive her to emergency and they take her from me. I wait on a green plastic chair and count the people that pass. They run a barrage of tests but can't find anything wrong.

X-rays, blood tests, CAT scans, ultrasounds, ECGs all reveal nothing. Then I can see her.

In a hospital bed she looks thin and old. The white sheets look heavy on her body, like they could push through

44

her, nothing but air. She says she has the taste of metal in her mouth, like something is leaching out of her salivary glands. It's as if she has been sucking on a copper lollipop, she tells the intern. They swab her mouth and give her lemon sticks to suck, but still the taste remains. The pain in her side is periodic and sharp. She describes it as a twisting knife. They suspect a problem with her bowel but when exploratory surgery is the last resort, Billie improves. When I say I will stay home and see that she is all right, colour returns to her cheeks, like the rouge she wears when she goes out.

Stress, the doctors say. *Just keep her company,* they say. I put off moving for another week and then sneak out like a teenager in the middle of the night when Billie has her black silk eye patches on and is snoring. I leave her a note and visit her daily for the first few months. She says she misses the dogs in an attempt to get me to come home.

Joelle and Pippa have found a small house in Fremantle owned by an old Italian family. It used to be a corner shop and the large lounge windows still advertise Bushells tea in fading, peeling paint: *Taste the flavour.* It is rundown and cheap to rent. In the summer evenings we sit in the lounge and open the two large corner doors onto the street. Outside, a few feet from the door, is a telegraph pole with the street signs attached, illuminated by the yellow glow of the street lamp. Traffic passes and drivers peer inside. We decorate it with second-hand furniture and street junk.

I'm good at keeping the place clean and I think they appreciate that. Mostly I keep to myself and they like my animals. I move in because they ask me to join them. If no one had ever asked, would I still be at home? Do I have any control over anything? I tell myself that I made the decision to move out. I move out so that I can get used to being on my own, prepare myself for life without Billie, and perhaps in the meantime some other kind of life might develop without my knowing. I see a new life engulfing me like amoebic protoplasm, softly folding itself around me without my awareness. Taking a more active part will be difficult.

And I do feel different here. The whistles of the port and the sounds of children in the nearby park are different from the sounds of Billie's house. Hers is the sound of the radio on low, like a conversation in another room, or the sound of television soap operas and police sirens on cop shows. Inside the Fremantle house there is sometimes pandemonium. Joelle and Pippa are young. Teenagers. They have friends and parties. There is music. Loud throbbing music that makes my room feel as if it is moving. I lie in the dark and listen to their lives.

I'm not considered overweight like I was when I was fourteen. Just a big woman. For a while I stop eating in a minor attempt to disappear and discover I do have a figure of sorts. I'm still not pretty or slim, and have given up on the image of beauty I had for myself (the one that rightfully should be mine if Alison is my sister). After school I never again wear a skirt, realising I'm at last free to cover my legs and therefore hide the mulberry-coloured birthmark that splashes across one calf. I have come to find its colour comforting, but only in my nude state does the blemish complement me; a stain that reminds me things will never be perfect.

So I am completely unremarkable in my looks. I am large and strong. I always wear trousers and loose shirts and cut my hair short. Billie hates my cropped hair probably more than anything, but has finally given up trying to persuade me to look different. I'm at home in my body and the clothes I wear. At the vet clinic clothes aren't important and almost no-one cares about make-up or nails. There is one female vet who says it's the worst job for a woman. She's always complaining about the animal hair on her designer clothes and the way she has to keep her nails short for surgery.

I don't call myself a vet nurse because I don't have the qualifications like the others, but we all do the same job and I know I'm as good or better than half the girls there. I'm the one the vets ask to help with the cranky dogs or to hold the feisty cats. One time a vet said it was like I oozed opiates. *Animals are calm around Cat*, she said, and the acknowledgment made me redden. This is the third clinic I've worked in and I've been here for years. My presence is the one stable thing in a practice that has a high turnover of staff. The animals recognise me. Once when someone commented on how long I'd been here I said, *I'm the all-weather nurse,* and remembered Ted.

1982. It's seven o'clock and time to go home when Paul says he has just had a call from a woman whose dog's fitting and frothing. Clare needs to go because she's got a *hot date* and Paul asks me if I can stay behind and help him. *It could be a poisoning,* he says and he's not dealt with one before. I wonder what they teach them at the university.

I tell him what I've seen other vets do over the year. I tell him we need to get it to vomit and then look at what it brings up. The Staffy arrives with long strings of saliva hanging from its jowls, all its muscles twitching and shuddering. Its body vibrates uncontrollably. Paul takes the woman and her dog into the consulting room and I lay out newspaper on the treatment room tiles so we can catch the vomit.

I set up the drip and everything he will need to catheterise the vein. I feel useful and in control. I wonder what he's doing in there. The woman leaves with a hanky pressed to her face, like she too is about to vomit. Paul leads the dog into the treatment room.

He gives it the apomorphine, placing a small tablet under the conjunctiva of its eye. It stands with its head down as a wave of stomach contractions pass over it. The dog hurls like his stomach is being turned inside out. A mush of shiny blue pellets. Snail bait. He keeps vomiting till all that is wrenched up is a teaspoon of orange bile. I pat the dog's brow and speak to it softly while Paul rushes around flicking through manuals and textbooks for more information. I can hear each book snap shut and another open. His shirt comes untucked from one side of his trousers and I glimpse his tanned skin. I suggest he ring one of the older vets but, after today's Lhaso Apso death, he says he wants to handle it himself. Show them he can do something right.

I hold the Staffy so he can put it on a drip. He can't find the vein. He pokes the needle around. Blood comes back then it blows. The dog moves and pulls back its leg. Three catheters are discarded before he gets the vein and the fluids are connected and flowing. I say, *Well done,* and I think he appreciates my support. He has started to sweat a bit and asks if the air-conditioning is still on. I tell him it is, but he can't feel it. His nervousness I interpret as caring. He gives the Staffy several injections through the drip and lightly anaesthetises it so the tremors stop and its eyes close. I keep a hand on its head and speak to it even though it can no longer hear me.

I put the drip bag between my teeth and carry the dog to an intensive care kennel inside the treatment room. I place it on a sheepskin and wipe some blue vomit from around its mouth. I sit down outside the kennel and hold its paw. Paul is ringing the woman and I can hear him explaining what he's done. His voice is deep and confident when he speaks to her. Now he sounds in charge.

When he's off the phone he comes over and leans down next to me. He puts a stethoscope to the dog's chest and lifts its lip to look at its gum colour.

Well now, it's just wait and see, he says.

Do you want me to stay with it? I ask.

Haven't you got to get home?

I tell him I've missed my bus and there's not another one till much later. He's apologetic and says I should have said something earlier. *No,* I say, *it's okay.* I wanted to be useful.

You were. I'll give you a lift. He says he'll come back later and check on the Staffy.

In the car I think about driving with Ted. He always found fault with other road users — a constant tirade of abuse about this or that driver. I tell Paul and he says his Dad's a grumpy driver too. *He's dead now,* I say, sort of jerkily and out-of-place. As soon as it's left my mouth I wish I hadn't said it. Paul simply keeps his eyes on the road and says, *I'm sorry to hear that.* I want to answer it's not your fault, but I say nothing. The silence is large in the car and I can smell mouldy material. I smelt it before when we were standing close and he was placing the drip and sweating. I think about his wet laundry in the machine, left overnight before being hung out. I think how the sun can't get rid of that smell. *Did you forget to hang out your washing?* I say.

You're kidding. You can smell that? I thought no one but me would smell it. Fungal flares. Ha.

I give him the directions as we make our way across a suburb to Billie's house. *My mother will be watching me get dropped off,* I say. *When I'm late she sits by the window in the bedroom and watches the street for my arrival. She's usually got the front door open before I'm even in the gate.*

He looks bemused. *What if a boyfriend drove you home and you sat on the verge talking in the car? Would she come out and search the car with a floodlight?*

Probably. Yes.

That night I dream about Paul. I run my fingers through his dark bouncy hair and as I think about him I masturbate. I bring myself to orgasm slowly and tentatively. Afterwards I feel guilty and sad. I end up crying, wetting my pillow with snot and tears. I wonder why the pleasure is so intense and sweet and then turns sour and bleak. I wonder if other people feel this way, but then I think how there is no-one I can ask. I might try and ask Alison if she was still here. But she left a couple of years ago and now sometimes it feels like she (and Dad) never existed. The time has swollen into an infinite number of long and silent nights without whispering and giggling. Without her stories of loving her boyfriend. Without her knowledge of our parents and the world.

The day after Mrs Teasdale's lawn, Alison and I are told we can help Mum prepare the provisions. Dad says he has a few lawns to do and will finish early to help get ready and load the car. I find myself looking at his penis that morning, as he prances his usual nakedness about the kitchen. I wonder if there is some way of telling if your father is being unfaithful by his penis. Does it swell with its newfound love? But this morning its shrivelled and fragile skin looks unchanged. Alison catches me staring and nudges me hard in the side. She shakes her head slowly at me like she thinks I'm a pervert. Ted doesn't notice me looking.

When Mum comes in he undoes her dressing gown tie and pulls her towards him as if to wrap them together within the one garment. I see how big his hand is in the small of her back, almost spanning the breadth of her. I watch her face to see if she's uncomfortable with his lustiness, but I think I see her smile meekly like she's grateful for his exuberant lasciviousness, even if it is in the kitchen and in front of us. I think, then, she has no idea about Mrs Teasdale.

We like shopping with Mum. Charlie Carters 1978. The aisles are narrow and often congested with pyramids of canned fruit on special. The trolleys are steel with small wheels that wobble and stick. There is a huge pile of brown cardboard boxes for shoppers to load up their groceries, and I think I'm really good at packing up our purchases. The only Parmesan you can buy is made by Kraft. It comes in a cardboard cylinder and smells like sick. We call it vomit cheese. We buy fruit and vegies from the greengrocer, not the supermarket. There aren't any fresh herbs except ordinary parsley, and there's only one kind of lettuce. If you want fresh fruit you can choose from apples, bananas, grapes and oranges, stone fruit and nectarines. In summer, watermelon and rockmelon are the treats.

At the supermarket checkout every item is laboriously punched into a large till by a woeful girl, required to dress neatly and have her hair tied back, who periodically dings a bell and asks someone to check on the price of a can of sliced peaches from aisle three. She knows Billie and cashes the cheque Dad has written out.

We buy our meat at the butcher where we've gone since we were little. He calls Mum *love* and always offers us a slice of polony, even though I have refused it for a while now. Lately the butcher shop has begun to repulse me. It has displays of tongues and sometimes a whole baby pig hanging in the window. I'm fond of pigs. He gives Mum salty-smelling bacon bones for soup, and large cow bones sliced down their length for Ben to gnaw on and then bury. He cuts meat for Mum right in front of her, on a table that is really a stump of a big old tree, crisscrossed with chop marks. He trims the fat, finally holding the steak up for her to inspect. *Oh lovely*, she says, and he pats it. It sounds like the slap of a baby's bottom, like it is alive. Then he wraps it in brown paper.

In the bank we withdraw twenty dollars each from our passbooks (saved all year from our pocket money) so that we have holiday money for ice creams and sweets, even though Mum says ten dollars would be enough. Billie doesn't have her own account. Dad is the supplier of money. Billie is in a good mood while she's shopping. She says Ted has given her two weeks of housekeeping money instead of the usual one and she feels like a millionaire. She buys me a Violet Crumble and Alison has a health bar, since she has given up chocolate, she says.

Ted is at home when we get back and I sniff him for the smell of Mrs Teasdale's Lux, but he smells of grass clippings. The blond curly fur on his legs harbours cut grass and grains of sand, and the hair around his neck and temples is dark and wet from sweating. He goes to give Mum a hug but she pulls away from his horse-like smell and says, *Have a shower, please, Darl.*

He says he is going to work on the car.

Inside we watch Dr Who fight the daleks while Dad works late on the car under the garage light. Through the glass French doors we can see him in an orange glow. Every now and then we hear him swear at the machine. He throws a spanner and we hear it hit the corrugated iron wall. The loud nostril exhalation won't suffice for machinery. They need a good talking to. No-one wants to be the one to tell him dinner is ready when we hear the commotion in the garage. Eventually Billie goes herself. We have ignored her and remained on the couch, our eyes not veering from the television in case she sees this as an indication that we are prepared to get him.

Inside he's fine. He's not angry with us. Billie did not do anything to the car and we kids can't be held responsible for a faulty carburettor. Tomorrow we are going to our holiday cottage.

After dinner Mum packs the boxes with the things we will need. She is organised and meticulous and I can see the similarity in the way she operates her kitchen to the way Dad is with his lawn mower. Does this make them compatible? I wonder if Mrs Teasdale has a spotless kitchen like Billie does. I begin to picture the other woman's kitchen, with filthy corners and the backs of her shelves sprinkled with hard black mouse droppings. I think, *How could he?*

When I get to work the next day, the Staffy is up and wagging its tail. His tail thumps the stainless steel. He has chewed his drip out and looks pleased with himself. I have a churning in my belly that's new to me; a nervousness that's different from the general awkwardness I feel from day to day. I have a feeling of intenseness, and the ends of my fingers tingle when I touch anything. I walk around the hospital, knowing it's too early for Paul to be here, but I can feel his presence all the same. The smell of mouldy clothes has become vanilla to my senses.

I am cleaning out the kennels. I squirt a fluorescent line of stericide over the wet concrete cages and then use a heavy scrubbing brush to cover the surface with greenish yellow foam. The smell seeps into me over the day so I end up smelling like an antiseptic hospital floor — my hair, my hands, my clothes.

He's standing behind me and says, *The Staffy's looking good this morning.* I turn and look at him. He smiles and then turns away and goes back to the main hospital building. His voice works its way inside me and I hear every word over and over. I try to hear things in his voice and see things in his smile that aren't there. I feel a desperate sad feeling after he's turned and gone. All I have is this little sentence with six words. I have the small smile too, and make as much of that as I can. This mixture of desperation and hope leaves me feeling hollow, and I immediately think of Billie and her bewildered state without Ted. I think how much I don't want to be like her and yet seem inexorably drawn along her path.

It's Friday, and in the afternoon the nurses and vets talk about having a drink at the local tavern, a place with green glass windows made from the ends of bottles. The pavement outside smells of beer and cigarettes. No-one asks if I want to come and I try not to take this the wrong way. It's not something you need an invitation to and since I've never gone before when they've asked, why would they think of me now? Perhaps they think I am religious or don't believe in drinking. I chastise myself for being too pathetic to go uninvited and instead I wonder about the tavern on the bus ride home. I wonder what people wear inside, whether the nurses change into short skirts and put on make-up. I imagine Clare's unblemished athletic calves. If I were there, how

I would stand? What would I order to drink? Would I lean on the bar or sit at the table? Would I fiddle with a beer coaster and eat too many nuts?

Billie opens the front door as I enter the squeaky gate. Everything about me signals my mood. My shoulders slump forward, caving in on my chest, and my head hangs like a dog scolded. Billie doesn't help my mood by bringing attention to it. Saying things like, *That young vet won't find time for a sulky puss like you.* She serves up her gristle stew and white rice. I have given up saying I won't eat meat. It's like being called Cat; something I will do when I have extracted myself from Billie. I pick around the food trying to find the bits of meat unattached to pearly white tendons and cartilage that refuse to be swallowed. The chewy stuff slides from side to side, avoiding my teeth and making me gag. Once these bits were dealt with by a warm-nosed Ben, sneaked under the table and snuffled up.

After dinner I find pleasure in washing up. It's a solace that I've inherited from Billie and we do it the same way. I use too much detergent so the sink is full of bubbles. The water is hot, almost too hot, and my hands turn a dark pink. I wash the glasses first, then the plates, the cutlery and finally the pots and pans. I think again about the tavern and then, nonchalantly, decide I prefer this. I scrub the stove to remove some food splatters and then Jif the sink surface. I use way too much water and even though I want to conserve it (for the environment), my need to use lots and rinse and clean and rinse again is greater than anything. As I work at the sink with steel wool, my shirtsleeve flaps and I think the noise is like wind in the spinnaker of a yacht on the Swan River. In the days when I used to walk Ben along the fore-shore on a Saturday afternoon while he chased the willy wagtails that teased him on the oval, I would watch the yachts and see the miniature people bouncing on the deck, changing sails and pulling ropes. They looked like they were battling with the water and the wind, not enjoying it at all.

As I continue scrubbing, the sink becomes shiny, almost like a mirror. My face is a warped shadow in its bottom. My hair hangs down limply on either side of my face and I think then that perhaps a haircut, short and boy-like, will give me a lift. I say to Billie, who is watching a wildlife documentary on the television, that I'm going to get all my hair cut off. She takes a while to answer, as if she is thinking about the best way to approach this rebellion. She says, *You'll have to do more than that to win that young vet's heart.* I decide never to let Billie see Paul, and never to mention him to her either. Already my image of him is defiled by her comments and I wonder if I will be able to conjure an un-Billied Paul in my dreams.

1995. Sharing house for a year. Joelle is at uni and Pippa is out shopping. I have the house to myself. The dogs are following me around. Their little feet patter and their registration tags jangle from their collars — a comforting noise trailing me up and down the hallway. Everywhere I go they are right there, as if attached. When they sense I'm staying put in one room they settle down into their respective balls, on their sheepskin or chair or old pillow. It's as if they want to be within a certain radius and outside that the distance is too far — they must get up and move closer. I can hear Sam's stomach squelching and Lois snoring. Lois and Sam are small black dogs with pushed-in faces and bulging eyes, rescued from the vet clinic. Both of them have lots of problems and I call them my disabled pets. They don't swim. Their bodies and heads are too big for their legs and the sea frightens them. Sometimes they jump in the froth of the small foamy waves, but most of the time they don't even get their feet wet.

After Ben I thought I would stay away from dogs that love the water. When I'm down at the beach and I see a dog swimming out over the breakers after a stick, I can hardly bear to watch. When the dog swims past the stick, having not seen it, I wonder if I should jump in and start swimming after it, before it gets too far out. Just as I'm hesitating, deciding, twisting and turning, looking for its owner and bellowing, the dog will turn, sometimes swimming in circles or duck diving dog-style, before it heads back to shore. Sometimes I yell at the dog owner; scream at them for letting the animal swim out too far. I stand in front of them and wave my finger in their face. Then my voice falters. They turn and walk away from me and tell me to mind my own business. They think I am the crazy dog woman of South Beach.

I'm fond of Joelle because she knows my dogs are more important to me than she is. She doesn't try to make me notice her and in return notices me more than most people do. She notices the dogs' new collars. With Joelle and Pippa, conversation is silly and random, not about serious disease and terminal symptoms. But Billie disapproves of the dogs, or at least of the emphasis I place on them. Her rejection of them was one reason for my leaving when they offered me this place. She had begun to say she would prefer them outside, that she thought they stunk. She said irrational things, like she could smell their old owners on them — magic pine trees and cigarette smoke. Our landlord doesn't know I have the animals and so, on house inspection days, I take them to work. It is a job to eradicate any sign of them before the real estate people get here, but they have yet to find out. I even hide the dog food in case they discover it in the pantry, although I don't think they are supposed to invade your privacy by looking in cupboards. And Joelle and Pippa don't mind.

A typical day, any year, any vet clinic. A woman and her husband come into the clinic to have an old dog put to sleep. The man is crying before he even gets to the reception desk, and the woman does all the talking. Her hair is long and grey but she wears it out as if she thinks she is younger. I know Billie would say that she should wear it up and have it dyed. The woman says she has an appointment but doesn't say what for. I look in the book and see it's for euthanasia. The dog can't walk and smells of urine. Over its hip is a red and hairless sore from where it has been lying or chewing itself. The dog is very thin. I can see the bumps of its ribs.

They haven't been to the clinic before. I take them through to the treatment room and ask them to lay the dog on the examination table and say, *We will take it from here.* The vet asks them if they would like to be with the dog. The man is still crying and unable to speak. He takes his glasses off and put his hand to his eyes. He signals no, and rushes to get out of the room. The woman has said she'll stay.

I help the vet by holding the dog's leg so she can give the intravenous injection. I see the blood come back, red and thick, into the syringe and lift my thumb for the vet to inject. The vet is saying it will be quick and painless and the woman is holding the dog's head and looking blank. She has tears running down her face. When the vet has finished injecting the solution the dog is already dead, but the vet goes through the motions of listening for a heartbeat before saying to the woman, *She's gone.*

The vet stands there listening to the woman talking about what a good dog it is and how good it is with children. She talks about it in the present tense as if it is still alive. The vet says, *Fourteen is a good long life.* Then the woman asks,

When will she pass away? The vet says, *She has gone already,* and says again that she checked for a heartbeat a few minutes ago and there was none. *Oh, I see,* says the woman, the dog's head still in her hands. The vet pats the woman's shoulder and the woman thanks the vet and leaves. The vet and I can't understand how the woman missed the moment between the dog being alive and dead. When things die, they die so quickly. They are different, so completely different dead from alive. And even though its eyes were still open and its body still warm, it was so obviously dead.

The vet says to wait a few minutes before putting the dog in a bag. She believes the soul needs a few minutes to leave the body. I wonder how long it really takes. Together we put the body in a heavy-duty plastic bag and drop it in the freezer. It makes a dull thud, the noise of dead flesh hitting the freezer floor. I wipe down the table where urine from the dead dog has leaked out. I think about asking the vet why she says such and such *is gone* rather than such and such *is dead.* I wonder where the vet thinks the animal has gone. I notice the way people skirt around the word *death.*

1978. The car is loaded with holiday stuff. I have got Ben's things — his dish, his towel, his lead. I am happy to be taking him and have been told he is my responsibility. Mum wants to leave him at Nanna Pearl's but I promise that I will do everything for him and keep him under control. He has a habit of becoming quite mad at the beach. Besides, Nanna Pearl is likely to forget she has him and leave her front gate open. She sometimes forgets my name and calls me Joanna. I don't know who Joanna is. I say he is too strong on his lead for Nanna Pearl and will pull her over the minute he smells another dog on the ground. Ted says we can take him. He thinks Ben's a good dog even though he never pays him any attention except to berate him. Alison has no time for Ben and says I shouldn't let him lick me on the face. But I don't mind his soft warm tongue.

Ben is dog-excited to be coming, and barking and jumping around the car. Dad raises his hand at him like he's going to belt him and he settles down. Dad puts him in the back with all the boxes and bags and he lies down with his chin on his paws. Alison and I have our pillows with us in the back of the car and Billie has a pile of magazines as if we are going hundreds of kilometres. Before we have even left the driveway she's offering us one of her sugar-coated jubes, and their sweet sickly smell is making me feel ill. I can hear her sucking and chewing on the soft jelly. I roll the window down a bit but Billie says it's giving her a draught on the back of her neck and asks if I can put it up again.

We have set off early *to beat the heat*, as Dad loves to say. He is suggesting car-riding games when we are still on Stirling Highway, and Alison and I just groan back. *I spy with my little eye?*

We cross the Old Fremantle Traffic Bridge and pass the Fremantle Maritime Museum. It is an old lunatic asylum. I think how I like the word lunatic. We pass the prison and I can see guards on the high-walled corners. I've been told there is broken glass set into the stone along the top and I imagine cutting my foot on it in an attempted escape. I think of the murderers inside and Mum says, *How anyone can live in Fremantle, I'll never know.*

Passing the Newmarket Tavern signals the end of Perth and surrounding suburbs and we feel we are away from it all as we pass Robb Jetty and the sheep yards. The skin-drying sheds on the right send out a stench of wet wool and ammonia, and I wonder if the sheep on the left side of the road, awaiting slaughter, can connect their fate with the smell of the sheepskins across from them. Even with the windows rolled up I can taste the smell in the back of my throat. A sharp, sad smell. The power station overlooks the water and the abattoir outlet. Horse trainers gallop their thoroughbreds on the sand and then swim them in the effluent-grubbied ocean.

We make fun of the shacks perched on the water before the Kwinana industrial area. We ask one another, *How could anyone have a holiday here under the smell of minerals and smoke and metal and gas?* The fibro shacks are painted assorted colours like fading liquorice all-sorts and have skirts of green mowed lawn around them. There's a stumpy tree or two and old broken chairs to sit on out the front or back. The chimneys and smokestacks of the refinery climb high into the air, and billows of dirty white smoke pour out of their tops. Mum says that when Alison was four and I was still a toddler we drove past the industrial area and Alison said, *Look Pollution*. This story is often recalled as an indicator of my big sister's innate intelligence.

The road is higher than the industrial sprawl, which spreads out on the shore like a giant rubbish tip with pipes and rusting metal buildings. We take the Mandurah Road and in the distance see the grain terminal poking out into the Rockingham water. Giant silos filled with wheat. There's a salt lake on the right and its crusty surface looks like you could walk on it. Horses stand about in brown paddocks, flicking their tails. Some have on light coats and eye shields. Billie says she thinks the car is making a strange noise and Ted tells her it's inside her own head. There are old stone houses with rusted machinery overgrown with grass and fields littered with dead trees.

A small sign and a petrol station mark the turn-off to Singleton. We go over a rise and can see the ocean. The settlement is small. There are shacks of all descriptions but they're still just holiday homes. People don't live here. The fibro cottages offer the bare essentials. They are pastel coloured — greens, blues, pinks and yellows. Some have asbestos roofs. Some have two storeys where the ground level is all just car parking and ping-pong and washing line. There isn't much in the way of gardens, just a bit of lawn here and there and an oleander or hibiscus, or an unpruned and straggly rose bush. The streets are all unkerbed and the bitumen just peters out into sand and gravel tracks. There are footpaths between the shacks making short cuts to the beach through the sides and backs of houses. The beach is just a beach. There are no flash amenities or car parks cordoned off with treated bile-coloured pine. There are no proper driveways or people with landscaped gardens.

The feelings I have for Paul, those tingly sensations I have when I hear him speak, start to fade as the weeks since the dog poisoning and his driving me home fall into the past. He still smiles at me but I can't make as much of it as I want. He gives me a few more lifts when I stay back late to assist. I say he needn't go out of his way. I make him drop me off on the highway. He pulls into the bus bay and keeps the motor running as I get out. The moment is over and the car has driven off before I have even thanked him for the lift. I see the back of his head silhouetted in the car as it leaves, but less and less do I imagine putting my hand on the curve of his neck. This way I feel less pain. I'm not nervous in his company and the smell of his clothes no longer arouses me. I wonder if it was a crush. I think I am fickle for feeling so much and then so little. Billie no longer makes her snide comments.

    In the evenings Billie and I have returned to our routine. I tell her about the cases I have seen during the day and repeat the things I hear the vets say. We discuss the animals' symptoms and invariably Billie thinks she has the disease that I am describing, despite the fact that because it's specific to dogs or cats she couldn't possibly contract it. I have taken to bringing texts home and reading about medical physiology and anatomy and disease. I'd like her to know more about her body and take some control of her symptoms. I describe the postmortems the vets have done, and how they say, with scissors poised, *Let's see if I was right.* I tell her about a blood-filled sac surrounding a heart so it could no longer keep beating; an eggplant-coloured spleen misshapen and bursting with grey tumours; a heart riddled with worms liked cooked vermicelli. Billie says I probably know more than the vets.

My hair is so short you can see my scalp. At night I run my fingers over it and like to feel the bumps and slight indentations in my skull. It feels like the coat of a recently clipped dog. The hair at the back of my neck is especially good to touch and I pretend my hand belongs to someone else as I caress it. Billie says I look like an Auschwitz prisoner.

Paul stays at the clinic for another six months before he announces he's going to the UK to work. The others seem to have known for longer than me and I just find out because there is a bon voyage card from Clare in the staff room. I read the card she has written and see the flowery way she has written her name with a little love heart at the end.

Paul sends us postcards with pictures of low stone walls and patchwork fields, of Buckingham Palace and London

Bridge. He's learning a lot and has found himself an Irish girlfriend who he intends to marry. I see Clare's face fall when she reads this. Another new graduate, also called Paul, replaces Paul. I realise the new graduates are all the same. They all need assistance with the practical stuff. They haven't been taught the simple things, like getting a grass seed out of an ear. I help the new Paul like I helped the old Paul, but I'm not drawn to his straight blond hair or his unironed clothes. He, too, talks about his sex life in the staff room with the vet nurses and they laugh at his stories.

The new Paul ends up going out with Clare and one day I walk in on them in the staff room. He holds her waist, her back to him, while she washes the coffee cups. She doesn't use detergent, just cold water, and I think how the cups won't really be clean. I must remember to rinse mine with boiling water before I make my coffee. He has his legs apart, on either side of hers. I feel like I did when I saw Billie and Ted in an embrace. That feeling of longing and jealousy and incomprehension. They both turn when they hear me behind them and say, *Oh, it's okay, it's only Cat,* as if they could have sex in front of me and I wouldn't notice.

1997. I drive with the dogs in my small yellow car down to Singleton. I think I will retrace our steps to remind myself of the journey and what it was like. Perhaps it will help me. I'm

at the Newmarket Tavern in five minutes and only the back
bar is open as it's being renovated. It doesn't feel like the end
of town. The sheep sheds have all gone and the air smells the
same here as anywhere. There's an out-of-place caravan park
with A-framed cottages on the right. Robb Jetty is going to
be developed. The power station is an abandoned building.
Some people say it should be converted to a hotel, others say
it should be knocked down. Torn plastic flaps at its long windows and it looks majestic. Not like a power station.

There are jet skis for hire at the once polluted beach.
The boat building business is booming. Cockburn Waters
and Coogee are housing estates with houses in salmon and
terracotta. A man sells wilting flowers wrapped in silver
paper under an umbrella at the side of the road. The police,
concealed behind bushes, step out and aim their radar guns.
The lanes of traffic are separated by a median strip planted
with dirty green trees and shrubs. Seedlings survive in
recycled milk cartons surrounded by dry sand. The shacks
before Alcoa are still there and still the same.

I take the road to Rockingham and follow a scenic route
that takes me past the blue and white grain terminal. I head
south thinking I will link back to the Mandurah Road
somehow. I go through suburb after suburb with names I
don't recognise. There is a huge Australian flag flying from a
pole in the centre of a large shopping complex. I sense the
beach is close by on my right somewhere, but I can't see it
or smell it. I see lots of small brick houses with different

coloured roofs, and gardens with kerbing and palms and smooth, smooth lawn. I go through Waikiki and Warnbro and get to Port Kennedy before my road runs out and the houses disappear. I smell cement dust and bitumen. I have to backtrack a short way and find a road going east. It takes me to the Mandurah Road and past the glossy entrance to Secret Harbour. I'm nearly there.

I almost miss the turn-off, since the sign saying 'Singleton' is small. The large sign is for Bayside Beach, a new housing estate piggybacking Singleton. The Singleton Beach road follows the same path as before but the rest is different. There are Norfolk Island pines running down to the beach and lots of new houses. Only half a dozen old fibro cottages remain, but none of them feels like it is the one. I drive round and round like a prospective buyer but I am looking for something long gone.

The water is flat, a pale turquoise. It beckons. The dogs are eager to get out of the car. We walk along the shoreline and I stare out. The water looks as if it could never be rough or unfriendly. I collect some saltwater to add to my bath and seaweed for mulching around the base of the rose bushes.

Back in the car I sit and look out across the water. I watch a couple walk along the beach, hand in hand. I'm reminded of Alison and seeing her walking with her first love. The woman bends down to pick a seashell from the sand and the man moves his hand up the back of her loose shirt. She turns to face him and they kiss, her face lifted

towards him. I feel like I am watching a movie, that familiar feeling I have every so often when I view other people.
Like they are faking it. Celluloid characters in a romantic
movie who are acting their emotions.

As we come over the rise and Ben sees the water he barks. We
follow the mud map Ted's friend, who owns the shack, has
drawn. Mum is disappointed when Dad says, *Here we are.* I
can hear it in her voice when she says, *Is this the one?* As if
she's hoping he will correct her or say, *Just kidding.* It's the
same tone with which she asks if I feel like I'm going to start
menstruating. As if I can possibly know how to answer her.

It's a one storey yellow fibreboard shack. It's a rectangle
with a slightly angled roof. It has the number three on it and
a Mexican wearing a sombrero slumbers under a palm tree
on the wall near the front door. There is a circle of green
lawn where the sprinkler waters. Otherwise the grass is
brown and hard. It prickles the soft soles of my shoe-
wearing feet. The windows are louvred. We unload the car
while Ted cleans up the barbecue round the back.

Inside the house smells damp; of old bread and wet
towels. Billie goes round opening up all the louvres, some of
which have rusted into their closed position and need to be
forced. She pulls back the homemade cotton curtains with a
repeating pattern of bamboo and snow-capped mountains.

The material is old and faded and one curtain rips from its rod as she yanks it back. I think she is going to start crying as she moans, *Oh, Darl.*

Ted is bringing in the boxes and putting them on the laminex table in the centre of the big kitchen. The room is wide and spacious and bigger than our kitchen at home. I like the way we will all be able to sit in here, together, and maybe we'll talk. We won't watch TV with our dinner on our laps while Ted tries to compete with the 'Blankety Blank' contestants. There's no TV in the almost empty lounge room — just a couple of sagging, mustard-coloured armchairs with wooden armrests and a three-seater couch.

The stove is dirty and years of baked-on food sticks to its surface. Billie asks, *Where is the Ajax?* She has pulled on her thick pink washing-up gloves that extend to her elbows. Ted is standing behind her and has got her by the waist. He says he wants her to relax and not start scrubbing the moment she sets foot in the place. She looks especially short with her shoes off. Her two-inch heels don't go on holidays or caravanning. Her small white feet look clean on the grass matting. She has bent over to lift up a corner of the matting. She says she thinks it has never been cleaned underneath. *It is a sand trap*, she says. Ted turns her to face him and lifts her up off the ground like she is hollow inside, or just a toy, and puts her on the bench top. He holds her face between his large brown hands and gives her a kiss on her forehead.

Alison and I are emptying the car and coming in and

out of the shack, our arms loaded with belongings. They seem unaware of us, even though the flywire door creaks and bangs as we go through it. I feel uncomfortable when I see Ted kiss her on the mouth. Not just a small dry kiss. His large lips take over her mouth. I see that they both have their eyes closed, as if to block us out. Alison takes me by the hand and says we should stay outside.

We head down to the beach with Ben on a heavy rope that is an old horse lead. He pulls and strains and I am carried along behind. We can smell the sea. The sand is fine and white and fills our thongs and makes our feet sink. The front lug of my thong pulls through as I try to lift my foot out of the soft sand. I stand on one foot, off the hot sand, while I fix it. Alison runs ahead and down the dune towards the water. She screams when she sees we have the beach to ourselves. It is only eleven o'clock and the sea breeze isn't in. The ocean is flat and calm. We dive in.

I hold my breath and duck dive as deep as I can, then do breast stroke under the water. I pretend I am Jacques Cousteau and I'm scuba diving. Blue shards of light strike the bottom. Azure tones, rich and deep. Streaks of light ripple through the water. My cells link to the ocean as if I am bathing in bodily fluid meant for my nourishment. Like the liquid of my mother's womb. I breathe the water as if it is air. Jade turquoise fluid. Wet and dry at the same time.

I pretend it is like this. Really my eyes are stinging and everything is murky. When I resurface the smarting in my eyes is more intense. My hair gets in the way and I wish I had an elastic band to tie it back. A wet strand, its end like the sharp point of a pencil, flicks me in the eye. The water is cold and as it circles my body I feel my small and innocent nipples harden like Christmas currants. I pull my bathers away from my body and look down at my breasts. I think they look mature submerged and obscured by the water.

Ben is barking at me from the shore and Alison has got out of the water to shut him up. She is walking along the beach with him, looking for a stick to throw. She finds a bit of driftwood and hurls it towards me. Ben throws himself in and dog paddles to it. He sees it and lunges towards it with his mouth open. I think he has swallowed water but he doesn't seem to notice. He turns around and heads for the shore with the stick in his mouth. He drops the stick at Alison's feet, begging her to throw it again. Alison is bored by Ben and wants to lie on her towel and sunbake. I have to stop him wetting her and flicking her with sand. I take him away up the beach.

We walk for ages. I walk along the edge of the water playing games with myself, like being as close to the water as possible without letting the lap of the waves get my feet. I look back and see my footprints being washed away, leaving only slight soft indents in the shore. I watch the ground and imagine finding a lost bottle with a love letter inside it. I find shells. At first I pick up nearly every one and think it's a beauty. As I find more I get discriminating and end up throwing a handful of now ordinary ones back to the sea. Now I'm looking for colourful fan shells. Dark reds and crimsons and purples. I wish I had a bag with me to hold them since my palm is full and I don't want to throw any of these away. I think they are special ones. I go back and find Alison sleeping on her towel. I let Ben run up to her and lick her on the leg. I notice how firm her buttocks are, how bony and narrow her ankles.

Six months ago. I leave the house while Joelle and Pippa are still asleep.

They had a late one. It was three o'clock in the morning when they got home and put on the CD player. Propellerheads. I heard Joelle tell the others to keep it down since Cat was sleeping, but no one took any notice. I heard a glass break on the wooden floor and a body thump the other side of my bedroom wall. I lay awake listening to sounds of their laughter.

The living room is quiet in the dawn. It smells of spilt beer, cigarettes and sandalwood incense. I think they lit the incense to disguise the other smells, but the yeasty smell of stale beer is stubborn.

I go swimming at the pool just near where I live. It is a still, grey day, at the start of autumn. It is raining softly even though it is warm. There are lots of people at the pool. It's a Saturday and I've noticed people like to exercise at the start of the weekend. Maybe they feel they can overindulge with less guilt after having had a Saturday morning swim. The water aerobics class is full and swim clubs take up three lanes. The water seems dirty, but it could be just the grey sky. There were school swimming carnivals here all week, so maybe it is the aftermath of all the kids. My body feels lazy. I haven't swum all week and I feel a muscle complain even as I pull on my silicone cap. As I swim I see a large bandaid at the bottom of the pool, the centre gauze blotched by the faded brown stain of blood. The sticky plaster flaps and wafts on the concrete bottom. Each time I swim over it, it catches my attention and makes me feel contaminated. There are dead insects floating around like miniature space-men disconnected from the umbilicus of their ships and drifting in the endless expanse of water.

I am in the lane next to the aqua aerobics and I watch the orange-peel thighs jiggle beside me. When the instruc-tor makes them run and jump they set up a turbulence that is hard to swim against and I feel like I'm in the ocean fight-ing the waves. They stir up the water and I can see bits of dead skin and unidentifiable swimming pool flotsam. I'm at the end of a lap and stop to let a faster swimmer pass. I take off immediately behind her and the bubbles from her kick, small and silver, make the water seem cleaner. I catch my breath in the deep end, and in the next lane I see another

woman turn and kick off from the wall. I see how black and
dirty are the soles of her feet. I push off. Freestyle.

I begin to feel soiled and unwell in the water and almost
lose track of my breathing. I snort some water up my nose.
It stings and burns and I have to stop mid-lap to cough. A
man behind almost ploughs into me. He sees me in time and
goes round. He's stopped at the end of the lane and I smile
by way of apology, but he doesn't seem to notice, or thinks I
am making a pass, so he ignores me and pushes off in a flurry
of extravagant kicks and white water. Small children are
being taught to dive off the blocks and they swim like tad-
poles under the water, their compact bodies wriggling and
spiralling. They pop to the surface like gas-filled balloons. I
see a yellow stream follow one of the children through the
water. I see an old man having trouble keeping his bathers
up. I decide I have had enough and get out even though I
haven't done the two kilometres I told myself I was to do.

I dry myself beside the pool and watch the other swimmers. I pick out ones whose stroke looks relaxed and effort-
less. Ones who don't splash, but slice through the water like
they're on top of it. I watch these swimmers and try to work
out what they do differently. I watch one man with a kick-
board between his thighs who pulls himself through the water
with his arms. He is going faster than the guy in the next lane
who flaps around, his arms like windmills and his body con-
vulsing as he struggles through the water. I think the poor
swimmer looks like a dying bird. I believe I am graceful in the

water. A bit like a sea creature that is cumbersome and ungainly on the land but swims with ease and poise. I liken myself to a giant sea turtle. My size is not a hindrance in the water. Sometimes I feel I'm moving in slow motion, placing an arm in the water, changing the water's shape imperceptibly, as if the water and I flow together, connected.

In the change rooms I strip off my bathers and rinse under the open showers. There is a smell of chlorine and wet concrete. Women's voices echo off the tiled walls and damp floors. I don't use the cubicles. I have adopted Ted's acceptance of nakedness. I think some women are offended by the blatant display of my body, by the way I move my bosoms about and soap up my black triangle. The mothers call their small staring children away. Others pretend I'm not there as they scurry into the cubicles to shower in privacy. I don't do it to embarrass them. I do it to show myself that I have accepted my oversized breasts, my square frame and my heavy straight legs with their mulberry birthmark painted across one half. I do it because Billie would die if she could see me in the showers. She would never believe there could be so much flesh on a girl. She would never believe that I could find it acceptable to be like I am.

I am assisting in a surgery on a bull terrier. It is a big strong white dog that has been vomiting for days. The owners say it eats all sorts of rubbish and the X-ray revealed a foreign body stuck somewhere in the bowel. The vet tells the people we must operate to remove the obstruction. The owners say he will be the most expensive dog in the street.

The vet makes a large incision straight down the middle of the dog to find where the muscles join, and cuts in between them. The dog opens up and shows us its insides. Its centre is red and pink and purple and the intestines push their way out of the wound as if there wasn't enough room for them. They are full of gas and even someone like me, who hasn't been taught what normal is, knows this isn't right. The vet reaches in and pulls the guts out of the abdomen and works her way through them, running them between her fingers like someone unravelling a bunch of sausages. She feels the obstruction. I can tell from the way her face changes and her eyes go big and her forehead all creased. The bowel is dark and speckled and some bits are even black and dry.

She puts the normal intestine back inside the dog like stuffing socks into a drawer. She brings out the gut with the foreign body inside and proceeds to remove the piece of offending bowel. I open more swabs and pour saline into a sterile dish and check the dog's gum colour, and then the drip. I tell her he's looking pale and she says, *Fuck.* Then, *Jesus Christ, what a mess,* and then, *Get me the suture and extra clamps.* She gets the bowel out, a few feet of dark purple and black bowel, and drops it into the stainless steel bin.

She says she has a good job for me and then tells me she wants me to take the bin outside, and a scalpel, and open up the bowel, and tell her what's inside.

I say, *Okay*, and the others look like I've volunteered for something they wouldn't do in a fit. *Put a peg on your nose,* says one of the vets. The smell when I open the bowel hits me hard across the face and makes me gag. Like garbage left too long in the sun. I hold my mouth closed and continue cutting. The bowel peels away from the foreign contents. It is cloth covered in bile and stained brown from the gut. I pick it out with the forceps and drop it on the concrete. I get the hose and spray the material till it is clean and I see what it is. It's a pair of little girl's underpants with a dainty floral pattern on them. I hold them up in the surgery for the vet to see as she is closing up the dog. *Little girl's knickers, swallowed whole.* We all laugh and the vet says the smell's going to kill her if I don't get rid of them soon. *Bag them,* she says like a detective at a crime scene, *and we'll give them back to the owners.*

The dog recovers well and is eating the next day. The owners don't seem surprised that it's underpants we have pulled from their dog's intestine. They say he has poohed out whole socks before. The vet says they mustn't let this happen again. Next time they might not be as lucky. The owner says if the dog is silly again, he won't be getting the surgery. He wags his finger at the dog like he thinks it will understand what it has done. *Maybe you should invest in a laundry basket,* the vet says raising her eyebrows. The man doesn't notice her sarcasm.

I remember when I am fifteen and staying at a friend's house overnight. She's the first girl who's ever asked me stay before and I'm nervous of doing the right thing. I am conscious of my manners and call the parents Mr and Mrs Peterson whenever they ask me a question. I say *Yes* and *No* instead of *Yeah* and *Nah,* and Michelle looks at me like I'm someone different. Her house has lots of levels and I like the feeling of going up and down the stairs. She doesn't understand how I can find the stair thing so entertaining.

She asks if I want to swim in their pool and so we put our bathers on and leave our clothes on the floor in her room. She has bikinis, but I only have the bathers I wear for school swimming, fading and thinning over my fleshy buttocks. I push my pubic hair inside the bathers and pull them down from my hips. We lie on the concrete around the pool and get hot before we go in. She can dive but I'm aware of the large splash I will make and instead lower myself down the steps. When we are out and drying ourselves, she asks if she can feel my birthmark and whether it hurts. As her fingers touch it she says, *Ugh.*

The Petersons have an Irish terrier, Mac. It is a little dog that runs with its legs straight and bounces in the air as if it has springs inside. We are lying, sunbaking our backs, when Mac comes outside with my underpants between his teeth. I spot them, large and white, and so does Michelle. *Mac's got your pants,* she says and laughs. *Why would he want those?* she yells. I chase him around the yard but he doesn't let me catch him. He is fast and turns quicker than me. As I run, my bathers ride up my bum. He lies down with my underpants between his paws and gnaws at the crutch. *Mum,* Michelle calls, *Mac has Cat's pants and he's chewing them to pieces.*

They give me another pair of pants to wear home. They say I can keep them, as if to have them back would be unsanitary. Michelle's pants are small and tight on my hips and the elastic cuts into the tops of my thighs. At fifteen I think there is something sordid about me that has made Mac eat my underpants. Michelle tells all her friends how Mac sucked the crutch of my pants like I have something contagious. I am never invited back.

I ask the vet if dogs do that kind of thing very often and she says, *All the time, Cat, all the time.*

Alison and I walk back to the shack and Ben doesn't pull as much on the way home. He is spent, and ready to lie all afternoon asleep on the grey wooden boards of the back verandah. He will snap at the occasional fly that bothers him, and snore softly. He will jerk in his dreams and move his mouth as if he is catching sticks. He will sleep like a good dog.

Mum is at the kitchen window when we come around the side of the shack. She is cleaning. She has covered the sink with Ajax and has already finished the stove top. She says Dad is having a snooze, and if we intend to come in we should keep it down or else stay outside.

I watch Mum working at the sink, her small strong arms scrubbing at the rust on the stainless steel. I look at her hair pulled up on top of her head. I thought she and Dad might have done it while we were at the beach, but then I think her hair would be ruffled. I see the way her apron is tied in a neat bow behind her, but the buttons on her blouse, which does up at the back, are undone. I think these were fastened before. Then I think Billie is the kind of woman who could have sex and not let it mess up her hair.

With her back still facing me and her head down, I ask her if she was my age when she first got her period. She thinks I am asking because I have started, but I quickly add that nothing has happened. She says I shouldn't worry and it'll happen soon enough. She says she was only nine and knew nothing about the facts of life. She was in primary school and thought she was dying. She says Nanna Pearl hadn't told her or Aunt Bette a thing. She says Nanna Pearl used to keep her away from school all through her period, and she had to stay in bed with her feet elevated. She says, *It was a filthy business.* She tells me I am lucky, being more informed than she was, with a mother not so highly strung as hers. But I think that Billie is just like Nanna Pearl.

I try to remember a distant conversation Billie had with Alison and me about the facts. I remember being given a thin, soft-covered book with drawings in it and being told to have a read and let her know if we needed any questions answered. Alison and I sat together on the one bed, our knees drawn up to our chests, and read the description of sexual intercourse. It was a shock to know that the man's penis went inside the woman. I couldn't quite believe that that was possible. I had heard kids at school say that that was what happened, but I had protested and said it was kissing that made babies. I looked at Alison to see if this was the first she knew of it, but her face didn't give anything away.

Do you think Alison and I know all we need to know? I ask Billie as she cleans the drawers, tipping their contents onto the table and wiping their insides with a cloth moistened with white vinegar. *Oh, you girls are well educated about sex at school. We never learnt anything like that.* I want to be able to ask her more about sex, more than just the physical mechanics (but that too). I don't know the words. I want to ask what it feels like. Does it hurt? She does up her back buttons like she has felt my eyes there.

She runs the tap in the kitchen sink and piles in the unused dishes and cutlery. She bangs and clatters them as if to say she can't hear me if I ask her another question. It's a signal to stop prying. She is washing the clean dishes and utensils because *you never know about other people's hygiene.*

She wouldn't feel comfortable using them until she was sure they were *Billie clean*. I want to ask her if she had sex before marriage. Was Ted her only one? How did she know it was the right time and he the one? Sometimes I don't know if they are in love any more.

1999. The same questions in 1978 as the ones I would ask her at thirty-five.

It is harder to be frank with Billie now than it was then. At fourteen I was shy, but the inability to talk to Billie has become ingrained. It is a habit we have perfected. We know how each other avoids; how to hold back. We are used to treading carefully around one another, as if this is the way to show we care. We talk about disease and illness, symptoms and cures. We rarely cross the boundary like we did that day outside Mrs Teasdale's house. I am thinking of that day a lot lately. How, back then, I missed the opportunity to know Billie better. She wanted to tell me about her pain, about her self-destruction, and I only wanted to tell her about my memory of the bleached hand. The moment is gone when I could have asked about Ted and his control of her. I could have asked what she grieved for. Was she missing him or was she mourning the life she had missed because of him?

Ted says he is taking us to a Chinese restaurant in Mandurah since Billie has worked in the kitchen all day and he wants her to have a night off. Billie says she hasn't anything good to wear. She didn't think we would be going anywhere special. It's unlike Ted to spend money on eating out. In Perth we never go to restaurants. Occasionally Ted brings home fish'n'chips, if Billie is ill or has a twelve-hour migraine. Billie has to be near death not to cook the evening meal.

Mum is reluctant to go. *Oh Darl, I look a fright,* she says. She wants to do her face, and wishes she had brought some good shoes (with heels). Dad sits in the car listening to the radio while Billie gets dressed. He honks the horn. I leave Ben inside in case he gets confused and tries to follow the car. I think I am the only one who cares about him.

The Chinese restaurant is full of other white faces. On the wall are pictures of Hong Kong from airline advertising posters. Dad says, *Cathay Pacific is the best airline.* He says the stewardesses are the most attentive. *They have the best legs.* I ask him when it was that he was on an aeroplane, and he says it's what he's heard, not what he himself has experienced. He says he's not been overseas. He doesn't see the point of travel. We have everything right here in Australia. Alison says Dad is a philistine, but I don't know what that word means. Ted says he has nothing against the Filipinos.

Dad orders the sweet and sour pork, vegetarian fried rice (for me), satay beef for Alison, and chicken and almonds for Mum, plus extra steamed rice. The waitress doesn't ask us if we want to use chopsticks, she just brings us the cutlery. The red tablecloth has white paper doilies on it. I fidget with the salt and pepper shakers, and spill salt. It's like fine white beach sand. I suck my finger and dip it in the miniature white dune.

The waitress opens the beer Dad has brought and Alison and I are allowed lemonade. Mum asks for a Brandivino and dry but they don't have any. Instead she has half a glass of beer. She sips it slowly.

Ted's not used to waiting for his food. Mum always has things ready the moment he wants them. He looks uncomfortable. He keeps turning around in his seat. He watches the waitress as she takes other people's orders to their table. He is staring hard, as if he thinks this will make the food come quicker. Alison tells him to relax. *It's not good for your digestion to get uptight,* she says. This reminds Billie of Nanna Pearl and how she believes that meal times are sacred. Billie says that she and Bette never ate on their laps and, even though they didn't have a father, Nanna Pearl was careful to make sure the three of them felt like a complete unit. Nanna Pearl says that eating in any frame of mind other than a cheerful one is bad for the digestion. She believes good health relies on good digestion and good digestion relies on mental health.

Ted is not listening while Billie talks about Nanna Pearl. He has his hand in the air and is trying to signal the waitress.

She doesn't see him. He stands up and almost knocks his head on the low-hanging paper lantern. *Excuse me,* he says. *Our food?*

Alison and I want to die. Alison gets up and says she's going to the toilet. Dad says, *You sit still,* but she gets up and goes anyway. I want to go with her, thinking Dad is going to be rude to the waitress. Mum just says, *Please Darl,* but it is barely audible. The small Chinese waitress asks Dad, *Something wrong, sir?* and bows her body ever so slightly. Dad sits back down and says he is just checking on our order. Behind the waitress another one appears with some of our dishes and Ted says, *Okey dokey, we're right now.*

The sweet and sour pork is an iridescent orange and glistens in its sauce. The vegetarian fried rice still has baby shrimp in it, but I decide to let it go, since telling Dad will only make his mood worse. I wonder if shellfish the size of shrimp are sentient beings. The satay beef comes out sizzling on a cast-iron plate. We start eating, except for Billie. Hers is the last meal to arrive. She doesn't care much for the other dishes and so sits with her plate empty while we eat. Alison asks her if she should check to make sure they haven't forgotten, but Billie says it will come. She eats some of my rice while she waits. Ted says, *About bloody time, too* when Billie's food is placed on the table, but the waitress either doesn't hear or pretends not to. I wish he had not said anything. I see the people on a table next to us look over and stare. Perhaps they overheard, or are they watching him eat?

He eats quickly. I watch as a large spoonful of rice topped with a piece of orange battered pork is raised into the abyss of his mouth. He chews like a dog, with a loud slapping of his cheeks. If I look at him I can see the bits of pink pork between his tongue and the roof of his mouth. I don't think he knows what a spectacle he is. His focus is on the food as he scrapes the remains of orange sauce over some rice.

Billie puts a small amount of rice on the back of her fork. She doesn't use a spoon to eat her rice. She chews her food carefully, as if she is counting each mastication. She has given up correcting Ted's poor manners but she keeps her head down at the table, as if she doesn't want to see him and be reminded of what a sight he is. He pushes his plate a few inches from him when he's finished and looks up to see that Billie has barely started.

I remember one time, when I am only eight or nine and we are heading off to our weekly dinner at Nanna Pearl's, Billie asks Ted if he will try to eat politely. She tells Ted that Nanna Pearl has said, *It is like having dinner at a pig's trough, eating with Ted. How someone with manners like yours can stand it, I'll never know.* Dad says Nanna Pearl is trying to turn Billie against him. *Why haven't you said anything to me before now? Are you ashamed of me? You support your mother over me? Which one? Which one?* He keeps shouting. It is one of the only times I remember hearing his voice raised at Billie. He says that if Nanna Pearl doesn't like his manners then we will no longer go to Nanna Pearl's, and if Billie says anything to him about it ever again we will stop visiting her mother's. He says he needs her support and if she downgrades him like that then how can he trust her. These days it's like he eats noisily just to show who's boss. Some kind of dare.

We don't eat at Nanna Pearl's any more. We just stopped going. She is seventy-eight but seems older, folded into a large red armchair with her tapestry beside her and the television on loud. I think she must be near a hundred. We visit with Mum on a Saturday or Sunday afternoon and we do Nanna Pearl's shopping. Aunt Bette says Nanna Pearl has Alzheimer's from years of cooking in aluminium pots, and when Ted heard he made Mum throw out all our old saucepans and buy stainless steel ones. He says he doesn't want to end up like her. Billie says that the worst thing about Alzheimer's is the way it has made Nanna Pearl forgetful of basic hygiene. She says it's a good thing Aunt Bette lives with her or she would never remember to bathe. She used to smell of lavender and vanilla. Now she smells of stale urine and sweet sherry.

The road back into Singleton is poorly lit and there are only a few houses with their lights still on. Our shack is in darkness and I think how maybe I should have left a light on for Ben. He's asleep inside the back door, his nose pressed to the gap under it, as if awaiting the scent of our return. Dad says I should have left him tied to the Hills Hoist outside.

Alison and I go to our room and lie on our beds. They have green chenille bedspreads and grey blankets folded at their bases. They are narrow beds compared to our beds at home, and they sag in the middle. But at least we have our own room and are not cramped into a caravan with Ted and Billie. The room has a faint odour of mothballs. Alison opens the louvres to let in some fresh air. I can smell the salt and hear the waves breaking on the shore.

Ted starts shouting, *I'll kill that bloody dog,* and I run out of the room to see what Ben has done. Dad is hopping on one foot with the other in the air. He has squashed dog shit hanging from his heel. *He shat in our room right by the door,* he says. I start to laugh watching him naked and hopping, his penis and balls jiggling in the air and the smell of dog shit pervading everything. Mum is saying, *In here,* and I can hear her running water from the shower. I go back into our room dragging Ben with me, and tell him he should stay in here or he's going to get a hiding. He sneaks onto the bed, little by little, and I pretend I don't notice.

I hear the shower spray and then the sound of Dad singing. It is deep and throaty as he attempts to mimic Dean Martin. *Everybody Loves Somebody Sometime.* I wonder if Billie is in the shower with him. More likely she is Pine-O-Cleening the floor where the dog poo has been.

Mum pokes her head around our door to check on us and I feign sleep. She doesn't see Ben stretched out beside me, half concealed by the scratchy blanket. I can hear mosquitoes and feel them biting my ankles. I am hot under the blanket. When I hear Billie's soft steps going up the hall to their room, I push it away with my feet. I whisper to Alison a few times before I'm sure she is asleep. The shower is off now and I hear Dad close their door. It's so quiet in the country, I think.

I let my hand slide into my pants. I lie on my stomach with my hand making a fist between my legs. I push my fist into my groin. I feel hot. I let my hand relax. I want to feel what it is like to have a penis inside you. I put one finger in, slowly and carefully. It is slippery inside and easy to do. I bring it out and lick it. It tastes sharp on my tongue. I move my hips about on top of my hand and push my fingers deeper inside. I pull them out and find a spot and touch it. Softly, slowly. I feel a throbbing in my groin. Am I groaning? I am aware of my breathing, loud into the sheets. Ben has woken up and gotten off the bed and onto the floor, as if disturbed by my movement. I turn on my side and look at Alison's body facing the wall. I watch the sheet over her, gently moving as she breathes.

1997. I still work at a vet clinic where people are frank about sex. I should know a lot about it by now. I don't think the others imagine anyone being a virgin at thirty-three. Breeders are always coming in to have their dogs wanked and the semen inseminated into a bitch that won't stand or else is too aggressive, or shy or panicked, to mate naturally. The vets don't seem to mind collecting the semen in a little glass flask. They chat to the owner while they hold the dog's penis. It seems dogs get excited easily and the vet doesn't have to do all that much. My job is to hold the bitch and pull her tail to the side so that the dog can smell her.

One of the vets is collecting semen from an old dog that has a heart problem. The owner says mating will be too stressful for the dog and so instead they have brought it in for artificial collection. The vet is going to freeze the semen so that they can use it years later when he is dead. The dog pants a lot afterwards and the vet has to listen to his heart with her stethoscope before she can check that the semen is still alive. She puts a drop of semen on a slide and looks at it under the microscope. She says it has poor motility and some of the sperm are swimming backwards. The vet tells the owners it's not very good quality, but they say to freeze it anyway. *He has good lines*, they say.

An old client, Mr Gillespie, comes in. His hair is whiter than before. His eyebrows sprout out from his forehead like a cat's whiskers. His wife died a few weeks ago and he has been left with all her dogs. She bred silky terriers. Little silver dogs who are always shaking and trembling. He isn't very comfortable being in charge of them. It was always up to Mrs Gillespie. He brings them in to get their nails trimmed and ears plucked, because he can't do it like she did. The dogs won't let him. He doesn't know whether he holds them too tight or what it is, but they snap at him. *She did all the dog things,* he says again. When I ask him how he is going I don't expect him to tell me the whole story like he does. He says, *It was an enormous shock when she died.* He tells me that they were out doing the grocery shopping and she felt a bit dizzy. *That's all it was. Just dizzy.* He says they always shopped together. He was one of those men who held the list and checked the specials. He says he wasn't much help. They dropped the shopping at home and went straight to their doctor because she was still feeling funny. The doctor took her blood pressure and listened to her heart. He said she should go into hospital and have it checked. The doctor said there was no need to panic but he wanted to be sure. So Mr Gillespie says he drove her to the hospital and they admitted her. Over the next few days he spent most of the time at the hospital, just popping home to feed the dogs. His son and daughter kept the vigil with him. She just deteriorated in front of them. The doctors couldn't find out what was going on. It felt like all the tests were being done but none of them was providing any answers. He said he was with her when she died. She squeezed his hand. She was dead in three days.

When he walked into the house, that first time after her death, he felt how big it was. The shopping was still unpacked on the kitchen table. Things had begun to smell and go off. The meat they had bought for the upcoming week had gone grey and he could see bacterial colonies spotting its surface. The butter had melted into a rancid lake at the bottom of the bag. He saw his wife's favourite biscuits and the breakfast cereal that only she ate. Having to clear away the groceries brought home to him how it had only been three days. But it felt so long since they had been shopping together. He said the dogs were frantic, running around to look for her. He said her oldest one, Trixie, still smells of her Boronia talcum powder when she jumps on his lap in the evening. He says he thinks he will have to get rid of her. She is too strong a reminder of his wife.

I visit Billie on my way home from work. I notice the bright orange 'Aged' signs around her neighbourhood, a warning to motorists, and see a skinny old man walking along the footpath, his mouth agape like someone still asleep. I let myself in. Billie is in a tepid bath with old teabags on her eyelids, the yellow Lipton labels hanging over each temple. I sit on the bathroom step facing away from her and tell her about Mr Gillespie. She says, *At least he had three days. You can do and say a lot in three days. I think about that sometimes,* she says. *You know people that say cancer is such a bad way to die? Well I don't think so. You can say goodbye. Sort things out. Ted never said goodbye. We never cleared anything up because we expected to have so much time together.* I tell her that Mr Gillespie still suffered shock when his wife died. But nothing can compare to Billie's. She's competitive in her grief. Hers is always the most shocking, the most wrenching, the most consuming.

1978. Alison wakes me up. She has her bathers on and is ready for the beach. She asks why I have Ben in the bed with me. And doesn't he smell? I ask her if she was eaten alive by mosquitoes in the night and she says they have no taste and leave her alone. I look at my bitten ankles and bend over to scratch them. I smell my fingers. Ben licks my hand, exhaling into my palm and tickling it with his whiskers. Alison says I have creases in my tummy when I bend forward. *You could lose something in those folds,* she says.

I can hear Mum in the kitchen. On holidays she cooks big breakfasts for Dad. The radio is on and the cricket has started. I can hear the familiar voices of the commentators and the background buzz of static on the old wireless. The bacon is sizzling in a pan full of yellow butter and Billie cracks the eggs one-handed into the frying pan. Dad makes the toast and tea. Mum has brought her favourite china teapot from home so the tea will taste the same. The pot pours an even flow of dark brown liquid and steam rises from its spout. Ted hands Billie her tea and she sips it while watching the pan.

I stand looking at them from the hallway. They move as if in a dance. Their routines are like the movements on stage of a well-rehearsed play, finally perfected. There is a touch here and a rub there, a look and a sigh. Watching them I feel a certain contentment with the ease of it. This is one of those moments when you feel your parents' love for one another as if for the first time. I watch them and see that they are intimately connected in their movements. Like they are the two bits of the broken eggshell. Their edges are messy, but they fit together to make a whole.

Alison pushes past me into the kitchen. It's as if the bubble has broken. They look different from how I just saw them moments before. Their movements have changed from flow to staccato. They knock and bump each other. A plate almost falls to the floor and the toast is burning. I feel as if I have imagined the previous moment's serenity. Perhaps I made it up, like hallucinating an oasis out of heat shimmer. Perhaps what I see now is my real family and the other one was just a mirage.

Ted is tuning the wireless. Billie asks Alison to have some breakfast. She says she is going for a swim and does Billie want her to drown by making her eat all that fat before swimming? Doesn't she know you're not supposed to swim for two hours after eating? The back door bangs back and forth on its spring and Ben pushes out with his nose to follow her.

I sit down at the table with Ted and Billie and eat breakfast too. The bacon is extra crispy and salty. I use it to wipe up the yellow yolk of the runny egg. I forget that the bacon comes from the pigs I am so fond of. I have a cup of sugary tea even though Dad says I should give up sugar. I see him watch me as I spoon the sugar into it. I try to block his view with my body by turning to the side. But I know he sees. He doesn't say anything but I feel bad knowing he thinks I have no self-control. The taste of the sweet tea isn't the same now that I feel guilty.

Ted suggests we all go down to the beach after breakfast. The air is still and the easterly that was rattling the roof has died down. The day is heating up. The light is bright and the sky a clear pale blue, like a worn sheet faded by too many washings.

Billie says she isn't swimming and Ted shakes his head slowly at her as if he can't understand. She wears long soft cotton trousers with a drawstring around her waist. Dad says she should wear her bathers but she refuses. She placates him by saying that she'll have a swim later. My bathers are old green Speedos and I get Mum to tie a hair ribbon around the shoulder straps at the back so they don't fall off my shoulders.

We walk to the beach as a group. I try to walk in the middle of them and take each of them by the hand but the path is too narrow and I end up following behind, looking at Billie's soft creamy feet and Ted's callused and thorny heels. There are other families on the sand under circles of shade cast by their umbrellas. The ocean is flat and calm. As I dive in it is cold and fresh. I feel my skin.

Dad dives in and snakes his way along the bottom holding his breath. He comes up almost under me and lifts and throws me down. I'm aware of how heavy I am out of the water and the large splash my body makes. We dunk one another and I try to get away from him but he lunges at me and grabs my ankle. I get pulled under and water goes up my nose. I come up gasping and then he pulls me down again. Alison comes to my rescue and jumps on him from behind. He throws her off with a twist of his body and turns to splash her. I swim to the deeper water and watch them. Alison's high-pitched screams end abruptly as Ted dumps her. He raises his hands in the air to signal enough, and Alison swims out to join me.

It's too deep to stand or to see the bottom so we tread water. I ask Alison how long she thinks she could stay afloat, but she dips away and under me. I can't see her and look all around at the expanse of blue. I start to feel it's too long to be holding your breath. I feel my heart beat speed up just a fraction and I swivel my head to see if I have missed seeing her resurface. Then she pops up even further out than I thought she would and I think I am stupid for having panicked.

Dad is swimming parallel with the shore. His strokes are strong and even. He turns after a few hundred metres and comes back. I swim some of the way with him but can only keep up for a short distance. I see his circular mouth open for air as he turns his head to breathe.

Mum is on her towel on the pillowy dunes. Ben is hopping about on the shoreline and chasing small ripples of froth that cross the sand diagonally. I go up to where Mum is and spread my towel out next to her. *Nice in?* she asks, but she isn't interested in the answer. She hardly ever goes in the water, and when she does she keeps her head out. She says she doesn't want to damage her hair. Alison says that dying your hair would be more damaging than the sea, but Billie says the salt is drying. I look at her through the triangle I have made with my arm as I lie on my stomach. I see the wrinkles, fine lines around her lips and eyes, and notice that she has powder on, like the dust on a moth's wings. I ask her why she is wearing make-up on the beach, but she says she isn't.

The warmth of the sun makes me sleepy and I snooze as the salt dries into white crusts on my back. My legs are covered in sand. I dream I am in the water and floating on my back — supported by the Indian Ocean — tons of it. I fall asleep and drift. I wake up with a start and gulp water into my lungs. I swallow more and more till they are heavy with salt and I sink down to the black ocean floor. But I have not drowned. Instead I start to extract oxygen from the water as if my lungs have evolved back and become gills. Suddenly I have a fish tail, scales of silver and blue and purple, and I am propelled through the water with a gentle flick of my tail fin. I swim along the bottom seeing clearly and brightly. I am stirring up small eddies of sand that look gold in the light. Other marine animals come up to me but I am not frightened by them. A black and white killer whale swims next to me and we arc and curve in unison. A dolphin replaces it and we swim to the surface and rise out of the water in undulating waves.

1998. We are given the morning off work to attend a funeral service for a client. She wasn't just any client. She had a place for strays and unwanted pets. She called it an Animal Hotel.

Sheila has forty-seven dogs when she dies. The vet clinic is now responsible for them and we must find them homes or they will be euthanased. In her will she leaves all her money to the clinic to care for them. A vicious German shepherd will have to be put to sleep since he won't come to anyone but Sheila.

She had a special way with dogs. Those that were impossible for most people, she could handle. She wasn't much good with people, and even worse with children. She thought children were to blame for the way many adults lost interest in their pets. When some people had babies they brought their animals to her, saying things like *We just don't have time for 'him' now.* She had a sign on the large gate to her property that said *No children beyond this point,* and when she rehomed animals she made sure the new owners intended to treat them like they did their children, or better. She preferred to give her animals away to childless people, whose dogs would take the place of kids.

After she dies we find out she had been sick a long time. She didn't like doctors and so had ignored the symptoms of her cancer till the mass grew so large that it couldn't be cut out or irradiated away. She died in a matter of weeks. She became thinner and greyer daily. I remember seeing her in hospital a few days before her death. She is no longer recognisable as the strong woman who visited the vet clinic and held the muzzles of aggressive dogs. She is dwarfed in the bed, covered by a hospital sheet that hides her skeletal frame. She holds my hand and I tell her about her dogs and the ones we have found good homes. But once Sheila is hospitalised, the animals and her hotel no longer seem to exist. The smell of dog hair and urine, cat piddle and pet food is hard to conjure surrounded by meths, tea trolleys and the muted sound of nurses' shoes.

In the days before she dies she no longer talks about the animals she has spent her life caring for. She is angry that she is dying. She is too young, only fifty-five, and not ready. Her mother is still alive. During my visit, a friend brings her a bush potion made by the Aborigines to cure cancer. She is supposed to sip it, says the woman, but she cannot raise her head from the pillow.

At the funeral, the staff from the vet clinic make up half the mourners. We meet her few friends and family. Her mother is in her eighties and can't see or hear. I go up to her and offer my condolences while she is seated in a pew waiting for the service to start. I hold her hands in mine and remember holding Billie's hands as we walked by Mrs Teasdale's. I see how similar these old woman's hands are to those of my mother, and I hold them gently like I held Billie's. I say I am sorry for her loss and pretend it is Billie

I am talking to about Ted. *I'm so very sorry,* I say softly, but I know she can't hear me. I see how her eyes are filled with tears but she is too old to cry, as if crying is too much effort at her age.

The service is simple and dignified. A woman from the Donkey Rescue Society gives Sheila's eulogy and tells us about her enjoying dancing and music. I try to imagine Sheila dancing and realise I can't. I think then that I didn't really know her. To me she had dogs and dogs had her. I didn't even know she had a donkey. The coffin disappears into the marble ground of the crematorium and we are offered coffee and tea in the other room.

That night at home I read the death notices to see what people have said about Sheila. There is the one from the staff at the vet clinic with my name in the long list of employees. The only other one is written as if it is from Annie, a donkey saved by Sheila. It asks that people wanting to bring flowers to the funeral donate some money to the Donkey Society instead.

Six months ago. When I come back from my morning swim Joelle and Pippa are up. They're at the kitchen table with the backgammon set between them. They have hot cups of apple and cinnamon tea beside them, and they sip them periodically. Joelle squeezes a dollop of golden syrup onto the side of her fist and sucks it, pulling her skin into her mouth along with the sticky stuff. Pippa and I used to think Joelle and her lovers covered one another with it, after having found it in her room, on her bedside table. Then we discovered she just liked to suck it from the back of her hand while reading in bed.

They look up as I enter but don't say anything. I smile a toothless smile, just twist my lips. I say, *You're up*, as if I hadn't expected it, even though it is late.

Joelle is running the ball of her tongue stud along her front teeth while she contemplates her move. The sound of metal on tooth enamel is unsettling and makes the skin around my neck crawl. Pippa tells her it's bad for her teeth and that it'll wear them away and make them sharp. I don't think she is aware she is doing it — like me with nail biting. I think about the syrup and tooth decay.

I remember it is the week I move in that Joelle pierces her tongue. She's ahead of her time. She does it herself with a large-bore hypodermic. Pippa faints. Joelle's tongue swells up so it feels like she has a baby's foot in her mouth. She can't talk — the engorged muscle uselessly immobile. I tell her to gargle warm salty water so it won't get infected and she sticks it out for me to check with the torch when it feels like it isn't getting any smaller. Eventually it subsides. Apart from chipping a tooth once when she bit down on the metal ball, she says she hardly knows it is there. Now it is part of her. The small bright silver ball that I see when she laughs.

When she opens her mouth and it catches the light, it is like a secret being revealed.

They finish their backgammon game and ask me about my swim. Joelle is rubbing her forehead like she has a headache. I tell them the water was filthy and I saw an old man losing his swimmers as he trod water in the deep end. I tell them how I saw the dark shadow of his pubic hair and the flesh-coloured bits in the centre, dangling like bloated seaweed. I say that I don't think he was aware that he was exposing himself to the goggled eyes of the lap swimmers. They laugh. They say he was probably perverted, maybe he's a paedophile and knew exactly what he was doing. I tell them they are cruel to think that. *He was just an old man with no elastic,* I say.

Joelle says her father will probably end up like that. At least she hopes so. She wants him to be so decrepit that he can't hold up his dacks in the water and there will be children spying on him from the deep and laughing. She hasn't seen him since we all moved out. Pippa says she should visit him for her birthday. *Maybe you'll get some money off the fuck.* I say I'll go with her if she wants some support. I'm interested to see what Joelle's father is like.

They tell me a story about the pool and why they only swim in the ocean. Joelle says kids used to climb the fence in the middle of the night after sniffing glue or taking speed. They'd run across the pool covers and the plastic sheets would ripple and wave as the runners bounced across the surface. It was like walking on water. A suspended brief moment of exhilaration coupled with the rebellious feeling of being on private property after dark. It was simple fun, till one night a boy slipped between a division in the heavy plastic pool covers into the unlit water below. His friends were too wasted even to miss him.

In the morning the pool attendants turned back the covers to find the body of the boy floating face down. Joelle had gone swimming at the pool the same morning and then heard about the drowning that night on the news. It sickened her to think she had swum in the same water that had drowned the boy. *Surely they should have closed the pool,* she said. She couldn't stop thinking about how he must have swum under the covers in the dark, searching for the gap, not knowing the surface from the bottom, swimming till his lungs wanted to burst. How eventually he would have simply opened his mouth and the water would have rushed in. Greedily. I tell them I think about that, too, when I swim in the ocean.

I wake up on the beach with a stiff neck. Billie has gone and Ted is sleeping on his towel beside me. He's only just come out of the water. His torso still shines with wetness. I have only been asleep for a short time. It felt like ages. I remember the dream. Usually I forget them but this one stays with me. I tell Ted about it, even though he seems asleep. His lips are parted slightly and his breath moves the hairs on his arms where his head rests.

At the end of my story he opens his eyes and says, *That'd be a good way to go, don't you think?* I say that I am worried about dying. I think about it a lot lately and worry about Nanna Pearl. He says he thinks Mum will fall to pieces when Nanna Pearl dies and we'll have to be strong for her then. He says, *Billie isn't a very strong woman, not like Aunty Bette.* I ask him what he thinks happens when we die. He says we get eaten by worms and that's the end of it. *I don't believe in any of that heaven mumbo-jumbo*, he says. *But you believe in it, Catrina, if that helps you. I don't mind.*

I tell him that at school we have learnt about what other cultures and religions teach. I say that the Buddhists believe that we get recycled. *They believe that the soul gets reborn into another body and just keeps going on for infinity. If we've been good we get a good rebirth and if we've been bad we might not even end up as a person but as an animal or insect, even an ant.* He says he can't imagine them getting someone his size into an ant's exoskeleton, and he laughs like he often does at his own jokes. But I am earnest. I say it is for this reason that we shouldn't eat animals. They may have been our mother in a past life. *Or father,* he says, and laughs again.

I feel the conversation with Dad was worthless. He doesn't take me seriously. He doesn't take anything seriously. I feel like balling my fist and hitting him hard in the stomach.

I imagine doing it and him buckling over. I feel my jaw tighten and my teeth press hard against each other. I feel like saying something to him about Mrs Teasdale. But how does a fourteen-year-old bring up adultery?

I look along the beach for Alison and see her as if she is a small bird way off. She is a black dot. I get up to go and join her. He grabs my ankle as I stand up, and says, *You should run to catch up with her. Might take a few pounds off if you tried a bit of exercise.* I blush at his acknowledgment of my size. My weight is pressing down on the sand as if I will just sink right through it. I feel leaden. I can't tell if it is a joke or not, and now I want to hear him laugh. He doesn't. This should be a joke, I think. I look down, past the mulberry stain, to his hand around my ankle and say, *Well, let go then.* I hope he gets sand in his face as I twist away and run off.

My running is languid even though it is as fast as I can go. Even the tears welling up behind my eyes fall in torpid streams down my face. I want to get to Alison and tell her what a wanker he is. She'll understand. I am hot and panting. I run into the water to cool down and fall into the pale blue. As I get closer I can see she is walking with someone. She is not alone. I start to slow down. I do not want to share her.

She is walking next to a boy wearing board shorts. He has thin straight legs and big feet that leave deep sand prints which fill with water like miniature lakes. Alison looks down at her feet after she turns and sees me running up behind. I think having a big fat sister embarrasses her.

She introduces Andrew as someone she knows from the school dance, but says no more. I walk along next to them but they are silent. I say, *Dad's a wanker.* Alison doesn't ask me what he's done. She says, *Cat shouldn't you put some sunscreen on your legs? You're going to go like a beetroot.*

I run off. Perhaps Alison will feel bad and come after me. I look back but she is still walking in the other direction with Andrew. I see the gap between her thighs as she walks. Mine rub together. He has taken her hand. Oh puke, I think.

I burst through the flywire door into the kitchen. My eyes have not adjusted to the dim interior and I can't see anything. I can still smell breakfast — the bacon fat and the burnt toast. It hangs in the air. Now that it has been consumed I remember its origin and feel sorry for the baby pig. I think it is the last time I will eat bacon.

As my eyes get used to the darkness I see that I have let in some flies. They move in straight lines and make ninety-degree turns under the kitchen light. Their buzzing seems especially loud, as does the hum of the refrigerator. The dishes and frying pan are stacked unwashed near the sink. It is unusual for Mum to leave them this long, but Ted insisted she go to the beach with us and do them later. I think I might do them for her. I wonder if she is in her room. I go up the hallway and look into their room. Their bed is tidy and flat. The tassels of the gold bedspread that covers it brush the floor. Mum has a framed picture of her wedding day beside the bed. She always brings this picture on holiday.

I think she must be in the bathroom and then I hear the shower start. I go to talk to her in the shower, like I did when I was little, before she stopped showing us her body. She looks startled when I enter, as if she doesn't know which part of her to cover. I see streaks of blood running down her legs. She turns to her side. There is no shower curtain to pull across. The white tiles look pink and the water swirling near the plughole is like rose-coloured cordial.

She says she scratched herself on some bushes coming back to the shack. I ask her if she is okay. She says, *Darling, give me some peace.* Her words are muffled by the shower. I wonder if she is crying. I am not sure if tears or water stings her eyes. I don't question how she could scratch her inner thighs, or remember she was wearing long pants. I think I want to tell her, *Dad said I was fat,* and for her to hold me. I don't feel that I'm too big to be cuddled; that if I sit on her lap it will look ridiculous.

I'm standing in the hallway just outside the bathroom when Dad comes back. I wonder if I will hear Mum collapse on the tiles. Perhaps it's menstrual blood. She is still in the shower and I can hear the water spray on the tiles. Dad is about to go into the bathroom. I stop him by asking where Alison is. I don't want to get her into trouble, but more of me wants to stop Ted from walking in on Billie.

He says, *I thought she was with you.* I say, *She's with some boy from school called Andrew.* He turns and leaves the shack to go down the beach to find Alison. Mum comes out of the bathroom and smiles at me. *Thanks, darling heart,* she says. I smile back. She hasn't called me *darling heart* for years. She looks clean and smells of gardenia flowers. I think then that the blood was an accident.

Outside my window I see Dad talking to Alison. She has her hands on her hips and is kicking the ground with her heel. The sun is straight up and they have no shadows around them. Dad is squinting in the bright midday light. He is pointing his finger at her while he speaks. I can see the vein in the side of his neck swell and his face is splotchy red. He has dark wet patches of sweat under the armpits of his Penguin shirt. I open the louvres to hear, and Alison glares over at me. I want to tell her I didn't tell him out of some kind of spite. I thought he was going to see the blood on Billie's legs and somehow I thought him seeing that would be worse for everyone.

Mum has gone outside to join them and says she has watermelon cut up inside and is making a salad. She's in a cotton dress with a big wide skirt that accentuates her small waist. It's an old-fashioned dress from the era Billie loves best. I think she looks like Judy Garland in the *Wizard of Oz.* She smokes a cigarette. Or rather, holds one. She rarely takes a puff. I wonder if the blood has dried into a fine line on her inner thigh. Alison is agreeing to everything Dad says with a half smirk. Billie stands back.

We eat the watermelon around the laminex table, spitting the pips first into our cupped hands and then putting them in a bowl in the centre of the table. Mum uses a knife and fork and works the pips out with the knife's pointed end. She has a thing about seeds. When she was young Aunt Bette had appendicitis, which Nanna Pearl blamed on the consumption of grape seeds. Ever since, Mum has refused grapes in case she swallows a seed. Everyone else uses their hands and has juice running down their chins. Billie is up finding napkins. I swallow the odd small black pip and immediately feel a twinge in my stomach. Nobody speaks.

1998. I have been living with Joelle and Pippa for four years. I'm used to seeing men, and sometimes women, come out of their rooms in the mornings. I'm no longer puzzled by the way the lovers touch one another, even if I am in the room, a dog on my lap. These days I don't always think of Billie and Ted when I see a couple embrace. And sometimes they touch me. Put a hand on my shoulder as they walk behind me to the sink, and I feel the warmth through my shirt. The visitor joins us for breakfast and herbal tea before leaving. Sometimes they are never seen again. But Hanif has become a regular.

He used to appear from Pippa's room but now it is with Joelle that he spends his time. I hear them giggling and

talking in the early hours of the morning before they fall
silent, and I imagine her curled into the arc of his body. He
bursts from her room, sometimes in one of her fifties floral
dresses, his long dark hair over his shoulders, and does a little curtsy to whoever is in the kitchen, as if we are waiting
to see who it is. People blossom from her space like butterflies from silk cocoons.

Lately he has stopped staying over and one morning I
ask Joelle what has happened. She says they have decided to
be platonic friends and study together, but refrain from sex.
I ask her if this is difficult for her but she says it was her idea.
He wanted too much commitment from me, she says.

So now, around midnight, Hanif emerges from Joelle's
room in his own clothes, his hair tied back and his buttons
done up. He takes a seat in the lounge where I'm sitting
feeding the kitten I am hand rearing. He watches me
intently. He comes up and stands behind me to see what I
am doing. I can smell Joelle's incense on his skin and as he
leans forward over my shoulder a loose strand of his hair
touches my face. I remember Paul for the first time in years.
Button has his eyes closed and is kneading my hand while
he suckles the teat. Hanif thinks it's amazing. He's never
seen anything so small and defenceless. I tell him about the
kitten and how it was found. He says he would like to rear
something one day — preferably a human being.

Six months ago. I spend the day in the small garden while Joelle and Pippa recover from their hangovers. They're not interested in plants or getting their hands in the soil. I remember watching Ted and Billie pottering in their respective garden beds — hers a clatter of wild perennials, his an orderly array of gerberas and annuals. I couldn't understand the pleasure they got from planting and watering or pulling weeds. I remember watching them, bemused, like Joelle and Pippa watch me.

I empty the wheelbarrow of the summer herbs that have died off. The basil has flowered and gone to seed. Its leaves have gone yellow and the stalks are woody. The end of homemade pesto till next summer. The rocket too. I pull it up and smell its peanut-scented leaves. The red-veined Swiss chard has grown larger than I imagined. No one liked it all that much. The soil looks pale and drained of its goodness. I have bought new soil. It's dark and rich and smells like a rainforest. I am planting bulbs. Ranunculi, freesias and tulips. Usually I miss the planting time and think of them too late when it has already turned cold. This year I plant early. Joelle says she thinks she hasn't the patience to wait for the bulbs to flower. I say, *The waiting is what makes them look so beautiful.*

I ask Joelle if she has thought any more about contacting her father. She says she doesn't want his money. I say, *I didn't mean about asking for money. I just thought maybe you would like to see what he's like these days. Maybe things will be different with him now*. I tell her I have been thinking about my father lately. I regret not knowing him more.

I remember how at fourteen Ted is unknown to me. I never have a real conversation with him. I think I love him, but only because he is my father. I think I am indebted to him and that somehow I belong to him. He makes me feel that I owe him something. I resent this. I feel as if I am struggling to break free of an enclosing egg, like a baby reptile that chews its way out and is off, scurrying forth immediately, independent and able to fend for itself. I would like to think I could be this reptile. I would like to shed skin after skin. Underneath I would be different, fresh and shiny, covered in birth slime.

I feel robbed that he's gone. Now we will never talk, even though I know his being here would be no guarantee of closeness. I think of the conversations I still don't have with Billie; of Joelle and her father. I think again of Mrs Teasdale. I decide to contact her. I'm washing my hands under the outside tap and talking to Joelle when this becomes obvious. I rinse the soil from my hands and watch it form a muddy lake on the paving. Suddenly Mrs Teasdale feels close by, as if she is just over the fence, a client in the vet clinic, or the person standing next to me while I select antipasto from the deli section in the supermarket. Why haven't I thought of this before? It has been six months since my walk with Billie.

I have another shower despite having had one earlier at the pool. I can still smell the chlorine on my skin and feel the tight dryness it leaves on the surface. I think feeling clean takes a lot of soap and water. I imagine that the water running over my body is washing away my anxiety. I revisit the memory of the creamy hand. I see the body attached to it; the light red hair, the smooth complexion.

It has begun to rain again and I think of the moisture seeping through to the brown-skinned bulbs. I think of them sprouting through the soil with their small green tips. I hold my head back under the spray of the shower. The dogs have followed me into the bathroom and sit and watch me. They watch the soap as it moves around my body, as if they think it is a treat I am about to drop them.

I put a leg up on the edge of the bath and wash between my toes. I see the grey soapy water spiral down the plughole. Their eyes look bigger as they watch my naked body. I wonder if they know I am naked. Does my flesh mean anything to them? But they look at my face, watching my eyes for acknowledgment of them. They don't notice that one breast is larger and hangs lower than the other. I remember Billie's small breasts and the pink water spreading out in rivulets down her fine legs. I step out of the shower and they lick the water off my legs. I lean down to stroke them and water drips off my nipples and onto their backs. They shake off the water and scratch at the door to be let out of the steamy room.

I walk to my room with a towel around me, leaving wet footprints on the floorboards. It is cool and dark. I have the biggest of the rooms at the side of the house. The others gave it to me since I signed the lease and I am the one who is always home. Pippa is often out all night and Joelle doesn't care about her room. My low bed is large and covered with quilts and doonas. The dogs are quick to jump on it and nestle themselves into a cosy spot.

I have a wooden tallboy and an old leather armchair in one corner. I have a discarded student desk, the type that has compass marks etched into its wooden top and a love heart pierced by an arrow. I think I must look large when I sit and write at it. I make up stories about the students who carved their initials into its pale surface. I have a string of Indian bells, a gift from Hanif, hanging near the window. They chime with the sea breeze. I put on an old pair of fawn corduroys and a faded blue windcheater and sit down with the phone book.

There are twenty-four Teasdales in the white pages and five around where Billie lives. There isn't one in Kinninmont Street. I think I will start with these five. What will I say to them? My heart speeds up as I write down the addresses and corresponding phone numbers. I feel my stomach turn over and I have to get up and go to the toilet. I feel like I am about to throw up. My hand is awkward as I push the numbers on the phone touch pad. I stop repeatedly before the last number, and practise what I am going to say with my French bulldog. She doesn't stir but keeps on snoring. My pug comes over and licks the back of my hand.

I will say, *I am looking for a woman called Mrs Teasdale who would be about sixty and lived in Kinninmont Street in the late seventies.*

The first one I try is engaged. The next doesn't let me finish before he says he's not interested and hangs up. I can hear children screaming in the distance before the receiver is banged down hard. The third says his parents aren't home. He sounds about twelve. The fourth is an old man who says his wife is dead but, *Yes, we lived in Kinninmont Street twenty years ago.* He says he doesn't enjoy recalling the time. I ask him if I can come over and speak to him. I say, *I think my father knew your wife.*

After lunch we play Monopoly. Alison is sullen. She doesn't team up with me against Dad as usual. Ted buys all the cheap properties and puts hotels on them. Alison's favourites are the most expensive dark blue ones — Mayfair and Park Lane — while I like the red and orange streets: the Strand, Trafalgar Square and Bow Street. The middle of the range properties.

Mum says it's too complicated, but the truth is, Billie doesn't like to play games. Aunt Bette told me Billie never played games when they were children, always preferring to stay on her own reading or sewing. Aunt Bette's mad on games and plays mahjong and bridge. She says games are good for the mind. While we play Monopoly, Mum sits with a book on one of the mustard armchairs. She crosses her feet at the ankles, since crossing your legs at the knees is why Aunt Bette has varicose veins as thick as electrical cords and as blue as grapes.

Dad insists on being the bank since he thinks that Alison and I can't be trusted with all that money. I end up in jail three times and have to mortgage my property to the bank before I have enough cash to leave jail. Alison has the get-out-of-jail-free card and won't sell it to me.

We play for three or four hours every afternoon of the holiday when the sea breeze churns up the water. It becomes a ritual I look forward to. Dad suggests we play after lunch instead of sleeping or listening to the cricket. Alison thinks she's too grown-up for board games. She plays reluctantly, like she would rather be daydreaming on her bed, down at the beach with Andrew, or else staring at her face in the bathroom mirror. I've noticed her looking at her reflection a lot lately. She doesn't stop even if I catch her looking. She just stands closer to the mirror, as if to block me out of view.

1999. I think of Monopoly as Ted's game, his gift to me. I remember his hollers of indignation when he landed on my hotel properties or Alison's gasworks and train stations, or when he couldn't get out of jail. I remember him leaning back on the kitchen chair and laughing at me when I was bankrupt. I remember him running his hand through his thick curly hair when he was losing and him holding his money in the air and waving it at us when he won. I remember him knocking the board by mistake and the tokens and houses and hotels being upended, the money landing on the grass matting floor and Alison and I scrabbling under the table to claim it as ours. I remember him playing with the shoe token. I remember him blowing on the dice in his closed hand and wishing for a double. I remember copying his technique, believing he was lucky. I remember thinking that being good at Monopoly was training for life and the fact that I was always losing a bad sign.

1998. Hanif is in the kitchen helping Joelle and Pippa prepare for the dinner party. They have made hommus dip to have with Turkish bread, ratatouille from my old Moosewood cookbook, vegetarian lasagne and a big salad with rocket and organically grown tomatoes. There are casks of wine and a baby's bath, rescued from a neighbour's rubbish pile, full of ice and beer.

I am sweeping the floor. I get down on my hands and knees with the pan and broom and brush the dirt out of the corners, behind cupboards and chairs. Joelle says not to be too fussy, like she knows I can't help myself. I see their feet, shoeless and perfect. Crawling around the floor I discover other neglected cleaning jobs and wonder at myself for having let the place go. The skirting boards have a layer of thick dust on them and I get a wet cloth to remove it. I wonder how the dust has accumulated without me seeing it.

The others have finished preparing the food and are sitting at the kitchen table passing around a joint. Joelle and Pippa know not to offer it to me since I don't smoke, but Hanif just turns and hands it to me without asking. I take the joint and see Joelle and Pippa look amused. Joelle is about to snatch it from my hand when I put it to my lips and take a drag. Immediately the smoke makes me cough and I pass it on. Hanif asks if I'm all right and offers me a sip of his stubby. I wave it away.

During the evening I watch Joelle and the way she moves her hands while she talks. She has peroxided her hair and looks a little like Marilyn Monroe. She wears an old petticoat as if it is a dress and a tatty singlet over the top. The black straps of the bra-like top slip halfway down her arms, teasingly. She smokes cigarettes one after the other, like she always does at parties.

The dinner party becomes hazy. One minute I am hardly aware of myself and then painfully aware the next. When I speak I feel as if my mouth is contorting into strange shapes and the words are coming out in slow motion. But I see and hear people laughing at what I say, so I think I must be doing okay.

Everyone has moved into the lounge and is either dancing to the music or getting more stoned on the couch.
Normally I would wash the dishes now so the sink will be
clean in the morning, but I don't even stack the plates. I
remain at the table, unable to move, and Hanif sits across
from me. I notice his hands. His palms are a soft pale pink
and the backs a dark brown. I wonder about the soles of his
feet. He lets his hair out and runs his fingers through it. I
think I can smell cloves and asafoetida powder emanating
from him, and I ask him if he can smell it too. Yes, he says,
it's his mother's cooking. *It impregnates everything.* I say I
like the smell.

He puts his hand on mine on the table; dark on pale.
He rises and I am drawn with him. He leads me through the
lounge and opens my bedroom door, looks back at me to see
my expression, and then continues. I think my face is blank.
Perhaps it is flinching.

I wonder if he knows I have never had sex. I wonder if
Joelle and Pippa have told him about me and he is doing
this for them as some sort of weird favour. Perhaps they said,
Poor Cat never gets any. Would you mind?

I am thinking all these things in a flurry. I'm worried
about my body and what he will think. I am wondering why
this is happening to me now when I have given up thinking
that sex with someone would ever be possible. I had thought
there would never be a time when I would summon the
courage and the will to lead someone in here and lay down

with them, but now it is happening, and I am not in control. It is someone else's boldness. I let Hanif lead me. I will wait and see what he does next. I think I will leave it up to him. I feel buoyed, like I'm floating adrift in a huge calm sea.

He undresses himself and then takes my hand again and together we lie down on top of the bed covers. He undresses me slowly and I help him remove my top and bra. I feel acutely aware that no one has touched my breasts but myself. No one has run their finger from my belly button down to my cleft. I'm surprised that his touch feels so different from my own hand. It is lighter and more caring. How does he know so much about me? I see his leg wrapped around mine, his dark skin next to the port wine birthmark across my calf. He puts a kiss on the tips of his fingers and then reaches down and runs his fingers over it. I feel his breath on my face and want to capture it.

Afterwards I don't feel guilty or sad, but afraid. I am fearful of his departure. I watch him sleeping, the sheet over his hip. I smell the sweet fragrance of cardamon on his hair. I put my hand on his chest to convince myself that he is really here, with me. I move my face close to his and the scent of cloves. Sam lies curled at his feet. Hanif wakes when the black dog starts licking his pink soles that hang out the bottom of the sheet. He puts his hand behind my neck and draws me towards him and kisses me. I feel like I am bursting.

I know the love we have just made does not mean we're in love. I know we won't spend a lifetime together. (If he goes deaf he will have a hearing aid. If I go blind I will have a seeing-eye dog.) But still I tell him I am afraid he will leave. That I am afraid of everything. He says, *Yes, he knows. But doesn't the pleasure outweigh the fear? When the pleasure outweighs the fear,* he says, *it's worth the risk.*

1978. A week into the holiday. The weather is turning. There's a cyclone up north and the sky becomes overcast and dark. It's humid and still. The clouds are heavy and grey as if they are full to overflowing but can't let go. There is a strange light about and we have to switch on the kitchen fluoro to finish our Monopoly game.

At night it starts to rain and the drops sound large and heavy. I imagine them falling in slow motion and splattering the roof like small water bombs, changing the light grey of the roof to a wet black, bit by bit. I lie awake listening to the sound of the rain on the roof. Alison sits up in her bed and asks me if I'm awake. *Can you hear the rain?* She says we should go and watch it on the water.

In our shortie pyjamas we sneak outside. The rain is heavy but warm and we are soaked through in minutes. Alison takes my hand, like she did when I was small, and pulls me after her. I think she has forgiven me for telling Dad about Andrew. The sand dunes look silver and blue in the dim light. As we climb one I feel the wet sand crack to expose the still dry, warm sand below. We run down the dune towards the waves' phosphorescence hand in hand, my heaviness pulling her thin brown arm. The water looks black and deep. Our laughter sounds loud and shrill. She writes *Andrew* in the sand with her foot and watches the waves wash it away.

She says she's kissed him. She says that last night she snuck out and met him here on the beach. She says one day I will meet someone like she's met Andrew and I will know what an amazing thing it is to be in love. I say, *Are you in love?* And she says she thinks so. She can't imagine what else it can be. She feels so incredible all the time. As if suddenly she is alive when before she was dead or hardly existing. She says she can't wait for me to discover it. *Do you think that it is what Mum and Dad have? Have you got what they have?* I ask. *Oh God no, not like that,* she says. *They're married. It's different for parents,* she says. *Andrew's parents are the same. All parents are like that,* she says.

We swim in the black ocean and watch the luminescent water lap our bodies. The rain pelts its surface. I imagine the sea level rising with the addition of the rainwater and wonder if its freshness will weaken the sea's sharp salty tang. I imagine a layer of fresh water sitting delicately on top of the saltwater, the two not mixing. We don't go out deep, where the water is thick and dark like syrup. We stay in close where we can see the shore and hold each other's hand. We take small jumps off the bottom and feel, for seconds at a time, that we could be pulled off and out by a bigger force than we could resist. It feels dangerous and reckless. It doesn't take long for us to become cold and for our skin to tingle. The salt is extra salty. I wonder if it will dry out my pimples. We come out of the water and the cool air prickles our skin. Our flimsy pyjamas stick to our bodies. We run, shivering, back to the shack.

1979. Ted has gone and we are living with Aunt Bette in Nanna Pearl's old house.

As the summer of '78 fades, so does Nanna Pearl. She dies as if to say she can't bear to see Billie go on like she is. Her Alzheimer's deteriorates rapidly and she dies one night in her bed. Aunt Bette finds her with her eyes open and her mouth ajar, her hands clawed stiff around the edge of the blanket as if she had died in the process of pulling it up. She hated being cold. Her face is glaucous. When Aunt Bette phones Billie and tells her, Billie just hangs up without saying a word.

Aunt Bette arranges Nanna Pearl's funeral without any help from Billie. Alison and I walk behind the hearse while it crawls through the cemetery. I watch my reflection in the shiny silver bumper bar. Our shapes are deformed. Even Alison looks fat. I pretend it is Ted inside the coffin and in my mind I bury him. I set the worms to work.

Billie is in a daze. After Nanna Pearl's death she spends

her time weeping or else looking through her photo album and whispering to the pictures of Ted. Sometimes she hurls objects at people who visit to offer their condolences. The front yard is littered with cracked vases and jars and shards of broken crockery. She even destroys some of her wedding china. People's sympathy is hateful to her. She says Ted is coming back and why cry over an old woman like Nanna Pearl — *What had she to live for?* She has discovered a temper that she has no control over.

But the house still resonates with the spirit of Nanna Pearl, and sometimes I think I see her in the kitchen when I enter from the hall. She has been dead six months and the memory of her wizened frame is clear. She stoops over the sink, her chest like a soup bowl, filling the kettle. She warms her palms over the gas burner as she puts the kettle on the stove.

Billie can't seem to keep it together and Aunt Bette thinks it is better for everyone if we keep out of her way. Aunt Bette says that next year, when Alison is at uni, I will have to go back and live with Billie. Aunt Bette says Billie needs someone. I agree to it, like imposing a sentence on myself.

Alison is in her last year of school and doing well in all the subjects she likes. She spends hours on essays and reading. She and Aunt Bette talk about history and politics and feminism. Aunt Bette lends her books. She climbs a small stepladder and brings down dusty volumes from the shelves near the ceiling. She cuts out clippings from the paper that she thinks will be useful for Alison's study. Aunt Bette is thinking of retiring but says the children she instructs are the reason she feels young. She can't imagine not being surrounded by six-year-olds. She says they have so much more to teach her.

Alison and I share a room in the old house, but it isn't like when we were little. Alison is morose with me. With Aunt Bette she is thoughtful and polite. Somehow when she looks at me I feel she is wishing I wasn't here. Like she is vexed by the large awkwardness that is me. That my voice is hurting her ears and that everything about me is wrong.

Alison goes out on the weekends and is allowed to come home at midnight on Saturday nights. She goes to the movies with Andrew, or else to a party with his friends. One night she comes home early and I am still awake when I hear her mattress sag and her muffled cries into the pillow.

I think she is crying about Ted and realise I have run out of comforting things to say. She says she wants to talk when she hears me roll over and sniff. She says she needs to tell someone, but I have to promise never to tell Billie or Aunt Bette. I agree. I'm grateful for anything she wants to tell me. A small part of me feels special and important, then scared that the feeling will be pulled away and lost again.

She says she is pregnant. She cries in parts as she tells me how she has made an appointment for an abortion at a clinic at the end of the train line. She says she has organised it all herself for the next day. I ask her if she wants me to come and she says she just needs me to understand. She says, *I can't have a baby now. I have too much to do. A baby would ruin my life.* I think I understand what she means. Sometimes I think I have ruined Billie's life.

When I come home the following day Alison is there and acting normal. I drop my schoolbag in the hall and follow her out into the garden. Alison and I go way down the back behind the tool shed and into Aunt Bette's chook yard. We enter the darkness of the laying shed and our movements disturb the hens sitting on their eggs. I can smell damp straw and wheat. Some birds leave their nests. They flap their wings as they jump down from the laying boxes and start fossicking around in the straw bedding. I pick up a warm egg and hold it in my hand. I press it to my face till the warmth slowly fades. Alison sits down on the straw gingerly, and I think she must have gone ahead with it.

She tells me how the admissions nurse asked if she had drunk or eaten anything in the previous six hours. Forgetting that she isn't allowed fluids she drank a can of Coke on the long train ride. It settled her worried belly. Because of the Coke, they make her wait even longer before they will anaesthetise her. She sits reading the abortion information sheet, worrying about all the complications they list. She imagines her uterus perforated, popped like an overinflated balloon. She imagines the abortion failing and the baby growing anyway. She imagines sterility. She imagines infection. She imagines death.

She is counselled by a large woman in tracksuit pants and a blue sweater in a room the size of a toilet, and given contraception. She tells the woman she feels stupid and dirty. *I understand,* says the counsellor. She sits in a room with other women waiting too, mostly older than her, some accompanied by men or their mothers or girlfriends, and watches television. The eyes of some of the women look red and puffy as though they have been crying for weeks. No-one looks at anyone else in the room. They all just keep their gaze on the TV. Every program is about babies and children.

She says the staff are kind. Weirdly jovial. A nurse holds her hand when she is anaesthetised and then someone else strokes her forehead while she recovers. She remembers being led from room to room, a nurse at her elbow, feeling the cool smooth vinyl under her bare feet. She recalls clasping the white hospital gown at the back, afraid that someone might see her bare bottom. She doesn't remember anything about the operation, just the loss of consciousness as they give her the anaesthetic and the dry mouth when she wakes up. She remembers talking nonsense to the nurse as she recovers, and a cramping in her belly.

She says they wanted her to be picked up but when she insists she has no-one, one of the nurses drives her all the way home. She makes the nurse drop her off down the corner. She says that the whole thing wasn't so bad but she wonders if it will feel worse later. She says she thinks maybe years from now it will ache more.

After the abortion Alison stops seeing Andrew. She never tells him about the pregnancy. She blames her increasing need to study for her final year exams, and spends more and more time in our room with her books. She doesn't often come with me and Aunt Bette to see Billie, claiming she has work to do. Aunt Bette doesn't mind her not coming. It's as if I am the one whose job Billie has become.

At the end of the year Billie starts to ask when we're coming back to the house. She says she misses our company. Alison says she wants to stay at Aunt Bette's till after the exams are finished. I end up going to stay with Billie on my own.

When Alison finishes school she gets accepted into the ANU. She takes a flight to Canberra and I imagine her forgetting about me. She phones infrequently and when she does I don't know what to say. I pass the phone to Billie or Aunt Bette and hear them laugh at the things she says. Aunt Bette says Alison is happy to be inland, away from the sea, to live in a small upstairs apartment and to theorise on the political world. She writes to Aunt Bette and says, *I love that there is no sea breeze and the only water is a silly lake.*

Billie and I settle into routine now that there are just the two of us. I attend school while she stays at home and watches television. In the evenings and on weekends I clean, disinfect, polish, sweep and sleep. I finish school and my average performance doesn't lead me to university like it did Alison. Billie sees a university education as a way of me leaving and doesn't encourage it. She says, *One brain in the family is enough.*

Instead she helps me get a job at a nearby vet clinic because she knows the receptionist. They used to cut hair together. I am grateful to her for getting me the job. Being with animals is the only thing that makes me feel loved and loving. I miss Ben enormously but I'm not allowed to mention his name. It's as if he never existed.

Billie is still often ill when I move back and she spends days in her darkened room. I don't know whether it's headaches or depression or just plain grief. I press my ear to the door and listen for her breathing. I hear her snoring. I ring Aunt Bette when she fails to emerge after three days, and Aunt Bette comes over and makes tea. Aunt Bette coaxes Billie out like she would a six-year-old with promises of candy and sweets. She whispers to her through the keyhole till finally Billie pads weakly across the floor from the bed and unlocks the door. They kneel like children in the doorway and Billie crawls into Aunt Bette's lap. Aunt Bette cradles her thin sister in her padded bosom, and I feel jealous of their embrace. I would like to feel the comfort of Aunt Bette's ample flesh. I would like to comfort Billie in my Ted-like arms. I stand watching the twins, feeling large and tall and far away. The room smells stale. There's not a hint of the gardenia scent of Billie's talcum that once filled it.

Slowly Billie improves and starts cleaning again. I can hear the hum of the vacuum cleaner as I enter the gate. The windows are see-through. She polishes the wooden furniture with eucalyptus oil and the antiques with O Cedar. The day

I come home from work and smell the polish, I am relieved. She says she has found a new walking route.

Six months ago. When Mr Teasdale says on the phone that his wife is dead I feel unprepared. I never thought that Mrs Teasdale would be dead. I feel silly for not even having thought of that. People die easily, I should know. Have I just missed meeting her? If I had phoned a year ago would I have met her then? She must have been ten years younger than Billie and so should be in her late fifties now. Her hair should be steel-wool grey. I just never thought. I have missed the opportunity to talk to her about Ted.

Mr Teasdale has agreed to meet me later in the day. First I will visit Aunt Bette and maybe ask her advice. Should I tell him I think his wife had an affair with my father? I think how Aunt Bette wouldn't contact Mr Teasdale and dredge up the past. If I ask her opinion I will have to tell her who Mrs Teasdale was. She might think it is just another reason to dwell. *Dwelling*, Aunt Bette believes, *is the cause of depression.*

Aunt Bette still lives in the lattice-covered house she shared with her mother. I still think of it as Nanna Pearl's. I walk up the path to the front door. It is straight and formal. The garden beds on either side are raked clean of leaves. The soil is dark like expensive ground coffee and I think Aunt

Bette has planted her tulips. I must remember to tell her about my bulbs. There are diamonds of light on the wooden verandah as the sun makes it way through the lattice.

I turn the doorbell but it doesn't ring. Aunt Bette thinks its ring is too piercing and so has taken off the metal dome. There is just a faint trill. I can tell she's heard it though. I hear the radio go off and a chair move on the wooden floor. I imagine her putting her hands on the armrests and concentrating to get upright. She is stiff.

I hear her coming towards the door and can see her shadow through the leadlight glass. She is happy to see me. She holds my hands and says, *Catty, Catty, come in.* She draws me into the dark hallway. The house never changes. It has an old lady smell. Crabtree and Evelyn talc, and rosewater. Nanna Pearl's tapestries cover the cushions and walls.

She takes me through into the bright kitchen with large north-facing windows. She goes about making tea and buttering a date loaf she made this morning. I notice how she spreads it in thick random clumps. Bright red jam in assorted glass jars cools on the sink. She says she cleaned the copper kettle with Worcestershire sauce this morning and holds it up so I can see it shine. I notice how clean the floors are.

The familiarity of Nanna Pearl's kitchen is comforting. The walls are butter yellow and the floor is terrazzo. Little jewels of colour. It is cool and hard. Nothing survives a fall onto it. When I was little I liked to play on the floor, imagining the orange and brown bits were islands and the blue bits the sea in between. There is a large wooden table covered in newspapers and magazines. Now that she has stopped teaching, Aunt Bette buys three or four different papers every day and reads them from cover to cover. Sometimes I catch her doing the children's page colouring-in competition.

We eat the date loaf sitting across from one another. She looks at me as if she's searching my face, and says I look well. She asks me about Joelle and Pippa even though she can't remember their names. (When I shifted in with them she was thrilled. She asked me if I was a lesbian, the word like a lolly in her mouth, and added, *It's okay if you are.* I thought how it would not be okay for Billie. I told her I wasn't.)

She tells me Billie has said she would like to learn to play mahjong. Aunt Bette says she thinks it will be difficult for her to learn but has agreed to try to teach her if she promises not to cry the minute Bette gets frustrated by her ineptitude with the game. She says she hasn't much patience these days for teaching people the intricacies of mahjong.

I say, *I can't imagine Mum playing mahjong,* and we both laugh at the thought of it. Imagine her hands reaching for the tiles. Reticent. Delicate. Her colourful nails amongst the hands of the other old women who don't bother with polish, who don't wear gardening gloves and have the dirt of weeding embedded in their cuticles. Her small legs swinging under the chair beneath her. Her mouth trying to work itself around the Chinese words. Pung and Kong. The others casual in polycotton tracksuits. Billie sitting so as to least crease her pleated skirt.

Aunt Bette says she spoke to Alison on the phone the night before. She is going to have a baby. She is twelve weeks pregnant, her stomach like a small inverted question mark. Suddenly I feel sad. I can't imagine her pregnant and happy. I can see her at sixteen telling me about being in love with Andrew and what it feels like. I remember the chook yard and her face stained with tears. I remember trying to give her a hug in the confines of the laying shed and knocking my head on a perch. I fell over and got chicken shit in my hair. We ended up laughing. I wonder if she has done all those things she said she wanted to do before having a baby. Aunt Bette says Alison has finally finished her doctorate and is going to have six months off after the baby is born. She has even said she might come home.

I would like to know Alison's child, I say. I would like to bath her baby in a pink plastic baby's tub and pour tepid water over its large hairless head. I would like to hold it under its armpits high in the air, above my head, and hear it laugh. I would like to blow raspberries on its clean tummy that smells of breast milk and Johnson's baby powder. I think it might be good for Billie to know that grandchildren do happen.

I think about all the things I know and don't know about babies. Heinz, teething, gripe-water, husks, playpens, nappies (disposable vs cloth), cradle cap, nappy rash, Ribena, bottle-feeding, dummies, first words, colic and reflux, Napisan and baby oil, crying for no reason, vaccinations and whooping cough, controlled crying and feeding on demand, cot death, stewed apple, Bebisols, high chairs and baby capsules, sleep deprivation and slow healing episiotomies, plastic alphabet letters and unspillable drinking cups, sore nipples and mastitis, vulnerability, big heads, no hair, Michelin legs, orange faeces, capable of drowning in an inch of water.

Aunt Bette knows Alison and me well. I remember feeling that she was our rescuer when she drove down to Singleton to pick us up and take us back to Nanna Pearl's. She arrived in a brand new Toyota Cressida, and I remember commenting on how great the new car was. It was a silver-green, the colour of fish scales. Alison looked at me as if I was mad. It was impossible to say anything without appearing callous or unfeeling. The only acceptable thing to do was to sob. My tears didn't come. I felt all wrong. I couldn't grieve and I looked at the others who were and wondered if they really felt anything. I thought people were making it up. Alison cried and people comforted her. They put their arms around her shoulders and folded her into them while I watched on. She had Andrew and his family. When they invited her over to dinner I imagined them all sitting solemnly around the large jarrah table while she refused to eat.

I don't ask Aunt Bette what I should say to Mr Teasdale.
I think it is up to me to decide. I wonder if he still has freckles. Do they fade? Tomorrow I might ring Alison. Instead I
tell Aunt Bette I came for gardening tips. I tell her about my
wheelbarrow full of bulbs and how they will look like an
impressionist painting when they flower.

1978. After Ted has gone. We sleep in a bunk bed on the
verandah since Nanna Pearl believes the fresh air will do us
good. I can't think how air will help. I hear the lap of water,
but it must be wind in the trees since we are nowhere near
the beaches. I get my period. Nauseating waves of stomach
cramps to produce no more than a teaspoon of clotted
blood. Nanna Pearl strokes my hair when I can't sleep, her
fingers cool and long. We stay with Aunt Bette on and off
for a whole year, only visiting Billie briefly, like she is some
other relative and not our mother. Billie wants to be on her
own with her grief. She protects it like a bitch with pups.
She lashes out at people trying to take it from her as if it is
all she has. Then she discovers sickness.

We start a new year at school and I feel awkward. How
to explain it? I ask Aunt Bette and she tells me what she and
Billie said when they were at school without a father. She
says I will find a way of telling my story, but this is what
they did: they pretended their father was dead when really

he had run off with another woman and was never heard of again. She says she told her school friends that her father had died protecting them from an intruder. He was stabbed repeatedly in the chest with a large curved knife that came right out through his back. His blood still marked the verandah, she told her friends, and when they came over she pointed to the wooden boards, stained red with blood from where her pet cat had died. It had dragged itself there after being struck by their neighbour's new car.

1978. Alison and I wake up to the noise of the wind rattling a bit of the shack's loose guttering. It bangs like an impatient visitor. I have to remind myself that we were at the beach the night before. I still feel warm inside at the thought of Alison being in love and sharing it with me. I'm part of something. I feel as if I dreamt it. But my pillow is slightly damp from my wet hair and when I suck the coarse yellow strands, I can taste the salt on them. Down by my feet there is a dusting of sand on the sheet. It feels gritty.

It is cloudy out and I think the storms up north must still be affecting the weather.

Dad is seated at the kitchen table. He has a newspaper open and his elbow on the table with his head in one hand. He is reading intently. His eyes are close to the print and his finger runs under the words. I think that way of reading makes him look like a dullard. The kettle is boiling away. He is reading about the cricket and the upcoming final test against the Indians. He says the traditional game is still the better one and he's not all that interested in Kerry Packer's mob playing one-day games under lights. *I mean, it's just not cricket*, he says.

I ask where Mum is and he says, *She has one of her headaches*. He never calls it a migraine, refusing to believe such things exist. He thinks that saying she has a migraine will somehow make them real and worse, more likely to occur and more reason for Billie to have them. Ted's never had a headache in his life, not even from a hangover.

Mum is in the dark bedroom with an ice pack pressed to her forehead. When I enter her room my footsteps feel too loud even though I try making them soft and quiet. She winces as I make my way towards her, as if each step hurts her head. Her eyes open slowly and she looks at me. Her face is red and puffy. I ask if she'd like a cup of tea or anything. She says she just needs some time in bed. She says she couldn't sleep because her head felt as if it was being skewered. *It's the change*, she says. *It's turning everything upside down. I don't know who I am any more.*

I think she is going to expand on this, and the part of me that wants to be her little girl forever doesn't want to hear it. I'm not used to her opening up. Besides, I don't want to know that she is vulnerable. That she is, as I have suspected, not coping. That she is falling apart, breaking down, cracking up, shattered. That she is not whole. I think Alison would be more able to handle the revelation. For her, perhaps, it would hardly be news. So I say, *Shall I get Alison?* and turn my back on her.

I think I just want her to be well. I imagine briefly who I would want my mother to be. I would want her to be louder, more enthusiastic, the kind of woman that laughs, that hollers and sobs, that gets dirty, that doesn't wear washing up gloves, whose hair is sometimes out of place, who butters the bread unevenly, who sometimes forgets to cook dinner, who can run, who drives while her husband is a passenger, who can leave the house without make-up, who didn't have a noise in her head, whose legs were straight and thick.

I think about the perfect father. He would be smaller and less muscular, he would not get cross and then sulk, he wouldn't swear at his tools, he wouldn't have to have the last say, he wouldn't have to be the bank when he played Monopoly with teenagers, he wouldn't toot the horn while he waited for us in the car, he wouldn't hold Mum so that it looked like he could crush her with a tightening of his grip, he wouldn't walk around naked, he wouldn't talk with his mouth full, he would think about religion and history and science, he wouldn't think I was fat, and the only woman he loved would be Billie.

I tell myself I will never be like them. I look in the mirror and say I am not related.

I leave my mother in her darkened room with the curtains drawn and I see my father slouched at the table. He seems unable to function with Billie in bed. It annoys him that his plans for the day have been upset. He wanted us all to go for a drive and he can't see why she can't take two aspirin and be done with it. *What's the good of an ice pack?* he says to Alison while she prepares Mum a hot footbath. *If she'd just take the medication we could get out of here.* He says, *Billie is just manipulating the situation with her story of a headache. Manipulating what situation?* asks Alison, but Dad says, *Never mind.*

Six months ago. Mr Teasdale lives in an old art deco flat on the highway. It isn't far from Billie's and I think how often I have walked past it on my way to the library. He is expecting me and opens the front door before I can knock, as if he was waiting, watching me walk up the driveway. He is older than I imagined. I think, this is how old Ted would be. I try to imagine Ted at seventy. I wonder if he would have coarse grey hair sprouting from his ear canals and hardly any hair on his head like Mr Teasdale. I think men with curly hair like Ted's are less likely to go bald. Mr Teasdale's face is pale orange, the colour of an apricot. His freckles have coalesced. The backs of his hands are covered with scabs and sunspots. I wonder what all the years of sun would have done to Ted's large hands. Maybe he would have died already from a malignant melanoma.

Mr Teasdale says he is glad I'm on time — he can't abide lateness — and I feel as if I'm in the presence of a schoolteacher (one unlike Aunt Bette) and am about eight years old. He says to follow him and he takes me through into the kitchen at the back of the flat. I trail his smell of musk aftershave. He is wearing his slippers and I think about how Billie never answers the door as if she's just got out of bed, or is ready to get into it. *It gives people the wrong idea,* she says. The hallway is jammed with bookshelves. Books and papers lie in all directions over and on top of one another. Their spines are bent and the covers torn. I think a man that treats his books so badly can't have been very careful with his wife.

I stand in the kitchen while he turns his back on me to face the sink, fills the kettle and puts it on the stove. There is nowhere to sit in the kitchen and so I stand in the doorway, feeling self-conscious that I am so much bigger than him. A shrivelled lemon sits on the windowsill and a line of black ants zigzags across a cupboard door. I wipe my palms on the front of my trousers. I watch him make the coffee and notice the inside of the cups look stained and dirty. The coffee is a grey colour. It tastes grey too.

In the sitting room I perch on the edge of an overstuffed chair with highly polished wooden arms. He offers me a scone he says he made himself. I say, *Not right now,* hoping to avoid having to eat one. I don't know how to begin but he starts before me, as if he had no intention of listening to what I've come to say. He says he never knew my father but can tell, after seeing me, that whoever he was, he was the one.

The one? I ask.

Let me tell you the story, he says.

He says during the summer of 1978 he feels his wife, Ellen, slipping away from him. She is preoccupied. He says they don't make love any more and he thinks she has lost interest in sex. As an aside he says, *Few women naturally enjoy the act. Some will always find it repugnant.* I find myself screwing up my face as he speaks. He says he doesn't push her to be affectionate. He thinks that if he lets her be, she will *waft* back to him. He talks about her as though she is a leaf, weightless and insignificant. He says she cries all the time. She doesn't tell him she is pregnant till she can no longer hide it. Of course he knows it isn't his child, but she tells him the affair is over, and that, if he accepts the child as his own, she will love him again.

After the child is born she gradually gets better. Sometimes she reaches out and touches him across the table at dinner. Just rests her hand on his forearm. He doesn't have much to do with the baby, Sophie, and her brown eyes are a constant reminder of his wife's infidelity. Still, he thinks they will make it and get back to being a proper family. It's all he ever wanted, he says.

He never asks about the father because it makes him so furious and, anyway, his wife refuses to say anything about him. The man becomes a blemish in the little girl's eyes. A small black spot on her tawny iris. The reason Mr Teasdale can't look Sophie in the face. Mrs Teasdale begs him never to tell Sophie that he is not her real father, but he thinks one day, when the child is older, she will reveal his name to them both.

But when the child is five Mrs Teasdale is killed in a car accident. She is picking the girl up from kindergarten when she runs a red light and hits another car. Mr Teasdale wonders if she was daydreaming about her lover. His wife dies at the scene of the accident, even before an ambulance can arrive. She is thrown from the car, since she hadn't been wearing her seat belt, and lies with her neck twisted on the footpath. He remembers collecting the child from the kindergarten teacher's house and driving home, while the child screamed uncontrollably in the back of the car. Several times he contemplated driving off the road into a power pole.

Mr Teasdale tells the story as if he has recounted it many times. Like he has rehearsed it. Like he has waited a long time to be able to tell it. I sit listening, hunched forward, amazed and intrigued by the story. I am bursting to know more of Sophie. Perhaps she is like me.

In return I tell him my story. My story about the pale hand seems childish and unrevealing. I tell him I wanted Ted to love only Billie. He nods. I tell him we are both looking for people that can't be found. I ask him if he remembers Billie, a small elegant woman who used to walk by his house in Kinninmont Street. But he says he never saw her. He says he will talk to Sophie about me.

I sleep and dream of meeting Sophie. In my dream she is Joelle — after all, they are about the same age. I reveal to her that I am her half-sister and she says she knew it. We embrace. We are hugging and then we are kissing. My mouth is open and my tongue is in her mouth. It finds her silver ball and rolls it over and over. Our teeth knock and we pull back laughing. She says she knew I would recognise her eventually.

I wake up from the dream and it is still night. One black dog has fallen asleep on my foot and it has gone numb. It tingles when I wriggle it to revive its circulation. The other dog is dreaming too. His little paws paddle and his eyelids flicker. I wonder if he dreams of swimming.

Dad is determined to go for a drive, with or without Mum. He tells Alison and me to get ourselves in the car and wait for him while he makes sure Billie will be all right on her own. I think Billie can't wait for us to go. I think having us in the house is pressing down on her. It's as if she can feel Ted's bad temper penetrating the thin walls; every flick of the newspaper page and every sip of tea.

I sit in the back with Ben on the seat beside me. The front of the station wagon has bucket seats and Alison is quick to take Mum's place to control the radio. Fluffy blue sheepskins cover the two front seats so that I feel closeted and confined in the back. It's like sitting behind two giant bears, but I'm not Goldilocks. I have no view forward. I feel like lying down on the seat and sleeping but I know that Dad would accuse me of sulking. So I watch the flash of the white lines on the centre of the road with my face pressed to the glass. I keep a hand on Ben, sliding my fingers into his yellow coat and feeling the warmth of his body. I think how easy it is to be a dog and have no-one's expectations to fulfil.

While Dad drives fast down the highway, I listen to the sound of the tyres on the rough bitumen and see the sigh of my breath fogging the window. I can't hear their conversation in the front. I can see Alison's profile between the seats, but I sit behind Dad and can only see the top of his hair. I think it's good to be in the safest seat, behind the driver. I feel detached from them, like in a bubble. What can they be talking about? I can see Alison laughing but I can't hear her.

We drive at a snail's pace around a new housing estate. Now I try to pay attention to what Alison thinks is good taste. Dad is talking about what he would build. He compares his and other people's cars, their boats, their fences, their pergolas, their bricks, their roofs, their choice of plants. I think how Mum would enjoy this.

On our way home we stop at a petrol station for ice creams. I want to stay in the car but Dad says I must come in and choose my own. He says I am unsociable. I think that it's normal not to want to socialise with the people in a service station. Dad starts up a conversation with the man filling the tank as if to make his point. They talk about the weather and the cricket scores. Dad stands by the car with one hand on the bonnet and the other on his hip. I think he looks like that bloke on the car program on TV.

Alison is in the shop looking at magazines. She says she might buy one instead of having an ice cream, and I think she has a lot of self-control. The service station man and Dad come in and stand, still talking, near the counter. I begin to think that maybe Dad knows him from before. They seem like good mates. The Shell man asks a girl, about Alison's age, to get down some cigarettes Dad wants for Billie. She stands on a stool to reach the top shelf and as she stretches, her fingers just touching the gold packet, her short denim skirt lifts a few inches. The man looks at the girl's thighs and then gives Dad an exaggerated wink. Dad says, *Good job you got here,* and pays the guy. She has legs like Alison's, smooth and brown.

We drive back to the shack. Alison has her head wedged in the magazine. Dad is listening to the cricket on the radio and I think about the girl at the service station. Ben is farting and looking surprised.

It is the middle of the night. A slice of moon shines through the louvres, making the floor pewter blue. The moon's glow is like the light of dying neon. I have woken up and can't get back to sleep. I don't know what disturbed me. I can see Alison's meagre shape under her sheet. I lie on my back and watch the ceiling. I think about touching myself.

I hear a murmuring of voices. I move in the bed slowly so as not to make a noise. I let my body rise off the bed, inch by inch, so the springs don't squeak.

I imagine I'm a cat burglar. I see my parents' door is open and their bed is empty, the floral sheet on the floor. I walk slowly, silently down the hallway and hear Billie and Ted's voices coming from the lounge. I stand unobserved in the hallway and watch them. Billie has her head on Ted's lap and her body is curled on the couch. He strokes her forehead where the skin meets the hair like he is comforting a young child. He is saying, *There there.* She looks so small and feeble. He has her head in his hand. She says she is scared. He says, *I'm here.* I move backwards, aware of how easily I could be seen by them. Ted looks over at me as I retreat down the hallway. He acts as if he doesn't see me, as if I am non-existent.

I lie awake waiting to hear their footsteps going back to their room. I don't hear them.

It's the second last day of our holiday and Mum has not been swimming once. Dad has called her a *spoilsport.* He says she has wasted a beautiful holiday spending her time inside reading or else complaining of a headache. After breakfast we all go down to the beach. There are clumps of drying, stinking seaweed along the shore, washed up from the unusual weather we'd had. The shape of the beach looks different. The water is a perfect blue, light and clear in the shallows, turning to azure in the deep.

I watch Billie slip off her long cheesecloth pants, expecting to see the cuts on her thighs. I don't see any. I see smooth tanned legs and wonder if it's a bottle tan. We run and jump into the water. Mum walks in slowly and stops at progressive intervals. Knees. Thighs. Stomach. She stops when she reaches waist level and drops under as far as her neck. She doesn't put her head under. She swims about with her head craned out of the still water, doing a paltry breast stroke and avoiding our splashes. We don't splash her because *It's Not Funny* and she will just get out if we do. Dad swims up to her and she swims away like a glossy gull afraid of a bigger sea bird. *There,* she says, and strides out back to her towel.

1998. A client brings a kitten into the clinic. She is walking her Border collie by the river when she finds a hessian bag on the shore. She sees something move under the wet material and the dog sniffs the bag. Inside are three dead kittens and one, miraculously, still alive. It is wet and cold, probably near death. She puts it inside her top and holds it to her body while she walks to her car. The dog jumps around her and she has to push it away. She feels the kitten's cold nose and feet moving against her skin. She doesn't like cats, she says, but couldn't let it die like that.

We say we will take it and the vet gives it to me with that look on her face. *Please, Cat, will you nurse it?*

It's only a few days old and needs to be bottle-fed. It can fit in the palm of my hand and has a round tight belly after its feed. Its eyes are shut and its movements are sharp and jerky like those of a blindfolded child. I have to help it go to the toilet by moistening a cottonwool ball with water and wiping its rear, in imitation of its mother's tongue.

The kitten has suffered a near-drowning experience. It opens its eyes at about two weeks old, but still can't see. Even though it can suck from a bottle it takes ages to learn to lap and eat on its own. It remains awkward and it never meows. I call it Button since it has pushed all mine. He kneads my jumper and sucks the blanket when he sleeps, like a child glued to the comfort of its thumb. I want to save him but at about six months old he starts to fade.

Button's breathing becomes laboured and he stops moving around. He won't eat and I have to feed him with a teaspoon. I get the vet to put him on a drip and we X-ray his chest. It is full of fluid that the vet says is from a viral disease. She sticks a needle through his chest wall and syringes out the straw-coloured stuff that is making it hard for him to breathe. She fills a stainless-steel kidney dish with the liquid and shows it to me. A couple of cupfuls the colour of murky tea form a stagnant lake.

I ask if it could be the river water he swallowed when they tried to drown him. *Has the breathed-in water seeped out into his chest to drown him a second time?* She says no. *Cat, it's a high-protein fluid that is a sign of the disease.* She says, *Some cats just get it,* and there's nothing she can do. She says Button will die and that *it is best to put him to sleep.* I cry irrationally for the longest time over the death of the kitten. I feel both weakened and strengthened by the purging of tears.

It doesn't last with Hanif. He is twenty-two and I am thirty-four. He is cool and good-looking while I am grace-less and large. He is serious about being with someone but I have grown rather used to my own company. I question his belief that two make a whole. I am good at being solitary.

The fear I thought I would feel at him leaving doesn't eventuate. After six weeks he says he thinks we should stop seeing one another, and I agree. After all, he has long-term plans he is pursuing. He wants children and things I don't think I want to provide. I think of Sheila and all her unwanted dogs. I say I want to raise a joey next and he asks me to let him know when I have one, so he can come by and see it. He says he thinks he will stay away from our house for a while, since he has exhausted all the women.

I never tell him about Ted and even though I talk about Billie all the time I refuse to let him meet her. Hanif thinks my relationship with my mother is like his with his mother. I see the way his mother stands behind him and rests a hand on his shoulder when he is seated at the table eating some-thing special she has cooked for him, and I know he can't possibly understand. I see the way he teases the woman and she blushes. I think maybe it is different for boys.

We remain friends and he comes to me for advice on relationships. I ring him when Button dies and cry ceaselessly into the receiver. I tell him about Mr Teasdale and my discovery of a half-sister. He wants to meet her one day and I tell him he is only allowed if he promises not to seduce her. It is not a serious promise and a part of me daydreams Hanif will meet Sophie and they will end up having café latté babies. Still, sometimes he lies down next to me, on my bed, and we sleep together without touching. He emerges from my room in a pair of my corduroys and a crumpled linen shirt.

The last day of our holiday. I take Ben down to the beach in the late afternoon. I walk along the sand and he runs beside me, picking up bits of wood and brown seaweed and then dropping them at my feet. The breeze is in. The waves are choppy and the water looks swollen and strong.

Alison and Dad follow me down while Billie stays to tidy before we leave. Dad says she is fussing for nothing but she wants to leave it better than we found it.

I throw a stick for Ben and watch as he jumps the small waves and swims out. He grabs it and returns. He shakes at my feet and wets me. I hold the stick high in the air and he springs from the ground towards it. I wade out till the water is at my thighs and he paddles out after me. I throw it as far as I can and watch as he heads towards it.

He swims over a wave and I think how good it is to have an athletic dog. He goes past the stick. I think he can't see it and will turn back any minute. I jump to see if I can spot him beyond a wave. He must be twenty-five metres out and still swimming. I call him and feel my voice turned back towards the sand dunes, pushed away by the wind. I call again. Dad and Alison are standing next to me and we all watch the water and the gold dog swimming inanely further and further out. Alison says, *What did you do that for?*

We all call him. He turns and starts coming towards us and then veers off again. *Maybe he can't see the shore,* I say. Dad says, *Bloody stupid dog.* He drops his towel and sunglasses near his feet. He strides into the surf. He dives under a breaking wave and pops up on the other side. As his arm leaves the water I can see his outstretched fingers, held widely apart, and his wedding band glints as it catches the last of the sun.

There are moments when both dog and man are obscured by the waves. Then they appear on top of the swell, suspended in the air. Dad is nearly level with Ben and I think he must reach for his collar soon. I can see the two heads. They are close together, but they are small now. I see Dad's hand in the air, raised above the surface, and think he is waving at us to say he has Ben. I wave back. I look over at Alison to see if she has seen him too. I am alone. I turn around to find she has gone up the beach to higher ground, as if to get a better view. Mum is next to her. They stand staring out with their hands shading their eyes from the setting sun. I think they have spotted the man and the dog. I think I will see Dad and Ben reappear over the waves and body-surf towards the shore. Dad will be laughing as he slides through the froth of the ocean onto the beach. I watch the water and the lack of anything defining on it. All I can hear is the sound of the ocean; the waves breaking and collecting themselves up again; the cry of a seagull hovering above me. Maybe the silver gull has a view of the man and the dog. I see the piece of wood, the one I threw, wash up on the shore and go to pick it up. It moves back and forth in the shallows before sticking to the sand.

The sun is sinking and the light has faded. The water is turning inky. The sky is fairy floss pink. It shouldn't be a beautiful sunset. I don't know how long it is since Dad swam out. I run up to the others. Alison says to ring the police and runs into the water and shouts, *Dad.* Her voice comes back to us. Mum is standing there with her hand over her mouth.

I run to the phone box to ring the police. I feel the gravel burning under my feet. I want it to hurt. I try to run faster than I have ever run before. I tell myself this is a test and running fast will make a difference. I am out of breath at the phone. I ring triple zero. I say, *Police.* I say, *My father swam out and has not come back.*

Stiff-suited policemen walk up and down the beach and point their torches out to the black sea. Their flashlights sweep cones and tunnels of light across the sand. Men's voices rise and fall with the wind, and every now and then I think I hear a dog bark or Dad call out. Someone tells Billie that the strong winds have made holes and channels in the sea's sandy bottom, and that the rips are unpredictable. She doesn't speak. We sit huddled under a grey blanket, our hands gripping one another's, feeling the sand become damp and cool under our bare feet. Then Billie takes us back to shack.

The future? Tomorrow or the next day I will meet Sophie. I will enter a café on Marine Terrace in Cottesloe. It has a Malibu surfboard and ceramic ducks on the wall. I will know she is there before I spot her. She will be at the counter ordering a flat white. I will see her curly blonde hair. When she carries her cup to a table by the window I will see Ted in the way she walks. She will hold her shoulders back and her chin slightly raised. She will see herself in me as I walk towards her. We will sit opposite one another and just stare blankly for the longest time. She will speak first. She will say she is glad to have made a breakthrough. She will say she never thought she'd be thanking her Dad for putting her in touch with her biological father.

In my rush to explain Ted's disappearance I will leave many things unanswered. She will have lots of questions. I will tell her that our father's body is never found and that Billie believed periodically that he was not dead. I will say how my mother turned slightly mad for a few years and thought she saw him in shops or heard him shout her name in the street. She thought he had washed up somewhere down the coast and perhaps had suffered amnesia, that one day he would recover his memory and return to her. I will tell her how sometimes Billie believed he had run off with Mrs Teasdale and how she walked by the Kinninmont Street house daily for years to see if he was there. I will tell her how his disappearance made him even larger and more powerful than he had been in life. I will tell her that her own mother wept at the memorial service held three weeks after my father's disappearance.

I will slow down and expand on things. I will tell her about him playing Monopoly and him swimming in the ocean, about his casual nakedness and his large hands. I will remember the way he held Billie by the waist and drew her towards him. I will describe things I thought I had forgotten.

I will take Sophie to meet Billie. I will be unsure about whether this is the right thing to do. She will be curious to see if Billie is anything like how she remembers her mother. She will want to know as much as possible about Ted.

When I tell Billie who Sophie is, she will not be surprised. She will do an unusual thing. She will hug her. She will say, *I want to see if you are his.* She will say, *Hold me.*

They will hug and I will stand there watching. Billie will show Sophie pictures of Ted and our holidays. Pictures of silver caravans and smoky barbecues, of Alison and me as brown as berries, of the shack and of Ben.

She will take her into the bedroom and together they will empty his side of the wardrobe. Sophie will offer to take the clothes to the Good Samaritans. Together they will fold the khaki shirts and pants that Ted wore to work, making neat piles on the end of the bed. Sophie will lift them to her face to see if she can smell him. They will smell of lemon laundry powder. Billie has washed them every week for twenty years despite their not having been worn. The colours will have faded and the material will be thin. She will open the camphor laurel chest and they will go through his old jumpers. Sophie will be given a favourite dark green jumper, still smelling of machinery and grass.

Six weeks ago. Alison comes home to give birth to her baby. I am surprised she has chosen us to be part of the process. It is so long since I have seen her that I am frightened I will not recognise her at the airport. That I will walk past her and she will see this as evidence of my failure as a sister. I watch for pregnant bellies emerging from the airport lounge and see one, large and orb-like. A man supports her elbow and I know this is not her. Alison is partnerless.

She is amongst the stragglers; the old and arthritic. Her face is puffy and she looks tired. I notice her thick and swollen ankles, not the remembered shapely legs. Still, I recognise her immediately. It's like looking in the mirror when I study my face anxiously. Her forehead is creased like a fingerprint copy of mine. She sees me and smiles instantly. Warmly. We embrace as best we can. Her hard rotundness keeps me at bay and I remember the outstretched arm and her advice on personal space. *This far.*

On the drive back to Aunt Bette's, where Alison will be staying, I tell her about Sophie and ask if she would like to meet her with me. She can hear the excitement in my voice, quivering and high-pitched, at the prospect of us discovering our half-sister together. I hear it too and wonder if she thinks me childish, naive. I don't tell her how I think it'll be. Like a rough sea suddenly calmed.

At first she doesn't believe me. I have to convince her that Sophie even exists. So I tell her I can show her Mr Teasdale in his grimy flat. She says the thought of meeting a half-sister panics her. Like when she was small and got chased by an angry black dog. Having nowhere to run to. Like she will discover too much of Ted she doesn't want to know. She says she thinks that maybe she will be up to it after the baby. She doesn't want to think about it now. All she wants is to prepare for the birth. An extravagant form of nesting, burrowing, circling. *I want it to be perfect,* she says.

In the weeks that follow, Alison grows larger and fuller.

Her breasts swell so they resemble mine and she complains about how heavy they feel. *They are dragging my whole upper body earthwards,* she says, and we laugh together at the way they sway when she walks. Her hair loses its lustre and she cuts it short in preparation for a baby that will pull and tear at it. She stops waxing her legs and the hairs grow back strong and dark.

Baby any day now. I knock at the bathroom door when I hear her softly singing in the bath. *Catty, come in,* she says through the steam. Her arched back faces me. I ask her if she'd like me to wash it for her. I soap up the flannel and run it over the smooth pale surface of her skin. Her body has softened; no more bony protrusions of spine and hip, but the soft curves of womanly, contented flesh. I'm amazed at the tightness of her pregnant belly, at the line down its centre as if it will split apart. I think of her as an overripe fig, about to rupture. She takes my hand and guides it under the bath water, to where I can feel the baby's foot hard against her insides. It taps its heel on the drum-like skin. I am here and waiting, it says.

In the lead-up to the birth I spend less time at home and sometimes even need to ring Joelle and ask her to feed my dogs. She says the house isn't the same without my presence, and I feel an urge to hug her and thank her for saying so. She says Pippa has a new lover and they never leave her room. *I'm all alone,* she says. *You have the dogs,* I say, and she thinks I'm making a joke.

I go home to walk them. They jump and twist and turn in their excitement at seeing me. Their bottoms wiggle. The Frenchie groans like she can hardly contain herself and the Pug piddles a yellow line on the floor. I tell them I'm sorry for the neglect and I think they understand. I'm attaching their leads when I hear the moans of Pippa in the middle of her orgasm. I wonder if a baby is being conceived.

Billie, too, spends less time at home alone in the company of soap operas. When I go over to Aunt Bette's she is often there, her head pressed to Alison's belly, listening for a heartbeat or waiting for a kick from within. She gives advice on what not to eat and drink. On what causes heartburn and indigestion. Oranges are good, capsicum is bad. Bananas for potassium and cranberry juice for the bladder. She knows how to prevent the stretch marks that have already run like road maps all over Alison's stomach and thighs. But Alison is oblivious. Billie talks about how she will need to protect her nipples from the suction of the needy baby. Aloe vera. I try to imagine Billie nursing and can't. On the subject of the birth, Billie reminds us how a Caesarean is by far the most preferable and pain-free option for the modern woman.

Aunt Bette, with no personal experience of pregnancy or childbirth, remains thoughtful and supportive. Anyway. Anyhow. But she can't help asking about the non-present father. She wants to know who he is and why they aren't doing it together. But Alison won't be bullied on the subject of the father. She refuses to answer any questions regarding him. I'm impressed at her strength and imagine myself breaking down in confession at the badgering of Billie and Aunt Bette. When she stands, her belly knocks the table and a glass breaks. I sweep up the pieces and vacuum the floor while the old women continue to pry. She says if anyone pushes her again about the father, she will go back to Canberra and have the baby there. *Not another word.* That is all she will say. I am reminded of Mrs Teasdale.

I imagine a man somewhere, the father of the child. I wonder if he knows about the baby. Maybe he parted with his seed like Ted, in a reckless, haphazard fashion. Did Ted have any sense of the baby Sophie that grew inside Mrs Teasdale while he holidayed with us, his already-made family? I think of Alison refusing to share with the father the baby that is part his. I think of the way I wanted Ted and Billie. Greedily. And how Alison did too. How I always felt she was given more than her half. How the leftover love felt like a small morsel. How there wasn't enough of our parents to go round. Not for any of us. How the two of them were inadequate and how the loss of one further diminished the remainder.

I wonder if Alison, on her own, will be able to provide it all. Perhaps I will be of help to her. I ask Alison why she has chosen to come home after so many years away. She says that being pregnant has changed the way she thinks about family. She believed she knew all about us, but now, about to have a child of her own, having us close is a craving she can't control. Like pickled onions and peanuts, unexplainable but sincere and real. She wonders if all pregnant women view their relatives in a new light.

We are at Aunt Bette's watching the evening news and about to have dinner when the baby signals it is on its way. Alison feels the warm fluid seep out over the couch. We monitor the time between contractions, as we have been taught to do. I massage her shoulders and go over the breathing commands. We let her have sips of water and squeeze our hands when a contraction passes over her. In the quiet time I ask her what it's like. *Like being impaled,* she says.

When I get her to the hospital she is examined by the midwife. They say she has only dilated a few centimetres and it'll be a while yet. I wonder if she'll be able to stand it much longer. She can't find a comfortable position. In the shower, on the bed, pacing the room. It is all the same. Unbearable.

After a further six hours of contractions, her cervix has dilated only another two centimetres. The midwife suggests a drip. Over the phone the obstetrician says he wants to intervene. *It's not on the birth plan,* I say. I'm protective. I want Alison to see how much I will stand up for her. I will tell them whatever she wants. I feel bloated from tea and irritated by the calming sounds of the rainforest on the tape player. She pats my hand as if to say it's okay. She can't speak. I wipe the moisture from Alison's upper lip with a tissue and she cries now at the thought of another contraction coming any minute. How is it they can be so painful and yet her body doesn't open up?

After she gives in to the drip, the desired, natural, drug-free birth plan becomes lost in the medical foray. She has been in labor for eighteen hours. An epidural is ordered, gas sucked on, an episiotomy performed and the baby manipulated out with something resembling a plumber's plunger and forceps like oversized salad servers. I hear them grinding inside her, the sound of metal on bone, and am thankful she can't feel a thing.

I'm shocked and distressed as the baby emerges. It's all covered in slimy blood and its face is blue. Will it know to breathe? I try not to look worried when I see Alison watching my face. I grasp her hand. Suddenly I am reminded of watching the ocean. I feel as if we are both remembering the moment. Looking out to the horizon and searching it for our father and seeing nothing but the sun's light being extinguished by the sea.

In my mind I question if the baby is alive. Its face is pinched like it's bothered by the light. It is still and suspended in the air by the enormous hands of the obstetrician. He holds the baby aloft like a trophy he has winched from the insides of my sister. I see the baby boy suck in his diaphragm and then open his red, gaping mouth and holler.

The noise is a relief. I'm startled back to the present. I think I hear Alison murmur our father's name. The blue cord from the baby's belly button, twisting like rope, still reaches inside my sister as they lay the baby on her deflated abdomen and she weeps.

In the hours after the birth Alison is blissful. The swaddled baby lies in her arms and she cannot keep her gaze off him. He dreams, his small fist clenched as if he is hanging onto something. Sitting beside her bed I feel redundant. My job is over and suddenly my presence seems to intrude. I tell her I will be back later and she holds out her hand to me. *Thanks Cat*, she says.

In the lift to the lobby I am alone. A soft, tinny muzak plays. I see my reflection in the sepia-toned mirrors on three walls and think how drained I look. Old. I see the creases on my neck, like deep cracks in pavement. When the lift doors open an untidy group of excited visitors barge in without realising I need to exit first. I have to squeeze out around them. I smell the sickly blend of their perfumes. They are laughing, carrying helium-filled silver and pink balloons, large soft teddy bears and flowers in terracotta pots.

For ten minutes I sit in my car outside the hospital, unable to drive, and listen to the radio. I imagine the announcer mentioning the birth of Alison's baby as if I've witnessed a miracle. I'm exhausted but don't feel like it's sleep that I need. I question Alison's decision to come home to have her baby. Why did she want us now when she hasn't needed us for years? How long will her craving for family last? I picture it dissipating like some hormone in its postnatal phase.

Or maybe she's the same as me, looking for a piece of herself that has been lost along the way. Sometimes it's so small it's hard to recognise its absence. Like the baby boy already clinging to nothingness having left his mother's womb.

I drive home past the ocean. I picture Aunt Bette and Billie on their way to the hospital, gleeful. I see Rottnest Island, a blip on the horizon. Beach-goers are packing up as the sand cools and the sun weakens. They climb into their cars still dressed in their bathers or else change, half-concealed by a gaping car door and a towel wrapped about them. They leave the sand pitted and chaotic with the indents of their footprints. The sea, though, is calm. It's smooth and almost purple, like silk has been laid across water. I am pleased to be going home. I will go inside and see my dogs, cuddle them as if they're children.

Acknowledgments

I would like to thank my editors at Allen & Unwin for making the publishing process so enjoyable; Annette Barlow, Christa Munns, Jo Jarrah and Kathleen Stewart all assisted me enormously with the final polishing of the book. I would also like to thank my agent Margaret Connolly and Liz for their support.

In writing this book I was helped by reading Eulalia S. Richards' *Ladies' Handbook* (1939). It's where I found out about the baths that Nanna Pearl subscribes to. I also used Barbara Lord's *The Green Cleaner* (1989) to find out about all the old cleaning remedies favoured by Billie.

While writing *Undertow* I attended a six-week grief counselling course run by the Cottage Hospice and facilitated by Margaret Colvin. It was a wonderful course, full of personal stories of mourning, loss and recovery.

Thank you to my writing friends, Shelley and Annie, who always encourage me. Through my involvement with Shelley James of Cliff Street Publishing I have grown immeasurably. I would like to thank Clare and Jo for reading the manuscript early in its development. Thank you to my good friend Sandy. Eva Sallis at Driftwood Manuscript Assessment services provided early and invaluable support. Thank you to Driftwood's anonymous reader who provided an extremely helpful appraisal. I want to thank Marion Campbell, my creative writing teacher, for her enthusiam and belief in my writing many years ago when she taught at Murdoch University.

I would like to thank all my friends who have helped me, both knowingly and unknowingly. I am indebted to my colleagues, clients and patients at Kenwick Veterinary Hospital. Lastly my love and appreciation to Graham, for always being there, and for reading and rereading and rerereading.